For Dan, Brian, Ellen and Annie

The Time Spell

JUDI CURTIN

PUFFIN

Pengu Group Manh 4, USA
Penguin Group anada M4P 2Y3

Penguin Ir n Books Ltd)
Penguin 4, Australia

Penguin Book – 110 017, India
Pen ealand

Penguin Books (2196, South Africa

Penguin Books Ltd, Registered Offices: 80 Strand, London WC2R 0RL, England

puffinbooks.com

First published 2011
001 – 10 9 8 7 6 5 4 3 2 1

Text copyright © Judi Curtin, 2011
Illustrations copyright © Sara Flavell, 2011
All rights reserved

The moral right of the author and illustrator has been asserted

Set in 13/20 pt Baskerville MT Standard
Typeset by Palimpsest Book Production Limited, Falkirk, Stirlingshire
Made and printed in Great Britain by Clays Ltd, St Ives plc

British Library Cataloguing in Publication Data
A CIP catalogue record for this book is available from the British Library

ISBN: 978-0-141-335025

www.greenpenguin.co.uk

MIX
Paper from
responsible sources
FSC
www.fsc.org   FSC® C018179

Penguin Books is committed to a sustainable
future for our business, our readers and our
planet. This book is made from paper certified
by the Forest Stewardship Council.

1

I lay back and closed my eyes. I could feel blades of grass tickling my neck. The sun was warm on my face. I was sleepy, after hours of sitting in the back garden doing nothing.

'I'm wasting my life,' I moaned.

Tilly giggled. 'I don't know about your life, but you're certainly wasting that ice cream.'

I opened my eyes just in time to see the lump of ice cream slipping from the cone that I was holding. I tried to grab it, but despite my efforts, it slithered through my fingers and on to the grass beside me. It sat there like a small, lost, out-of-season snowball.

In temper, I squished the cone in my hand and then threw the whole soggy mess into the hedge.

Tilly continued to lick her ice cream into a perfect, neat sphere that was never going to topple anywhere.

'Why do you say you're wasting your life?' she asked. 'I'm having a lovely time.'

I sighed. 'It's the summer holidays and all we do is . . . stuff. We get up in the morning, do stuff, we go to bed and then the next day we get up again and do some more stuff.'

Tilly used her tongue to press her ice cream deeper into its cone.

'Well,' she said. 'I like the stuff we've been doing. We've been shopping, we've been to the beach, we've been to the park and we've gone for loads of cycle trips. We've been to the cinema a few times. We've been bowling. We've –'

'But that's all just us having a good time.'

'And the problem with us having a good time is?'

I felt like thumping her. 'There's nothing wrong with having a good time,' I said. 'But basically that's all useless stuff. We're young and we're smart and we have nothing to show for the last few weeks. What have we done that's important?'

Tilly was now nibbling the upper edges of her cone with her perfect straight white teeth.

'How can the two of us do anything that's important? We can't invent a magic food that will put an end to world hunger. We can't persuade all the armies in the universe to stop fighting. We're only twelve, remember.'

'Stop being so sensible,' I said, before realizing that someone who could eat an ice cream as carefully as Tilly was never going to be anything except very, very sensible.

'Anyway, I *am* going to make a difference to the world,' she said, ignoring me. 'I'm going to work really hard at school. Then I'm going to go to college and become an environmental scientist. I'm going to find a way to reverse global warming. I'm going to save the planet.'

How sensible was that?

'That's very noble of you,' I said. 'But that will take forever. And I don't want to wait forever. I want to make a difference to the world now.'

'Well, I'm delighted to hear that.'

I groaned.

Why did my mum always have to sneak up on people? Didn't she know when a conversation was supposed to be private?

'So, Lauren, you want to make a difference to the world?' she said.

I nodded cautiously, knowing there had to be a catch. When my mum is around, there's always a catch.

'Then you can bring this parcel to the post office for me,' she said. 'It will make a difference to your cousin John because he'll get his birthday present on time, and it will make a difference to me because if I don't have to go to the post office, I can watch the first episode of that new reality show that's starting this afternoon.'

I groaned again. My mum is addicted to reality TV, and helping her to watch more of it *sooo* wasn't the kind of difference I wanted to make.

Mum continued. 'I hope John likes his present. I love getting presents, but I hardly ever do.'

'Poor Mum,' I said, laughing. 'Nobody loves you.

4

Maybe you should go on a reality show yourself and you could make a few million new friends.'

Mum pretended to be hurt and I pretended not to notice.

'Well . . . get a move on!' said Mum.

'I have to do everything around here,' I protested. 'Why don't you ask Stephen or Amy?'

'You know Stephen's much too small to go to the post office on his own,' said Mum.

I sighed. My little brother is nine, but he's Mum's pet and she treats him like he's a baby.

'And I suppose Amy's washing her hair again,' I said.

Mum didn't answer, so I knew I was right. Amy is fifteen, and she spends her whole day washing her hair, putting on make-up and listening to really bad music.

Before I could say any more, though, Tilly was on her feet. She delicately put the last sliver of ice-cream cone into her mouth.

'No problem, Deirdre,' she said. 'Of course we'll go to the post office. The walk will be good for us.

Come on, Lauren. This is your chance to make a difference.'

I made a face at Tilly, but she ignored me. She was busy smiling sweetly at Mum, and Mum was busy smiling back at her.

'Let's go,' I said sulkily.

'I like your hair, Deirdre,' said Tilly, not moving. 'Did you do something different with it?'

Mum patted her hair.

'I got it cut yesterday,' she said. 'But you're the only one who's noticed.'

I pretended to get sick. Mum and Tilly have this 'best friends' thing going on that sometimes makes me totally crazy.

But mostly, I try not to care. You see, Tilly's mum died when Tilly was a baby, and how mean would it be of me not to let her share mine occasionally?

I took the parcel and the money from Mum and followed Tilly through the side gate.

One day I'd show them all.

I *would* do something amazing.

Then they'd be sorry that they didn't listen to me.

 **2**

On the way home from the post office, Tilly took a turn leading away from our house.

'Where are you going?' I asked, like I didn't know already.

'To the park. Let's go on the climbing wall.'

'But that's *soooo* boring.'

'Come on, Lauren,' she said. 'We haven't been in ages.'

'We were there yesterday,' I said.

'Well, it feels like ages to me,' she said. 'And you know I need to keep practising.'

I should mention that Tilly's a bit obsessed with the climbing wall. She thinks that when she's older, in her spare time from sorting out global warming, she's going to climb Mount Everest and raise loads of money for charity.

I decided to appeal to her sensible nature. 'Climbing's dangerous,' I said. 'You might fall and hurt yourself.'

She laughed as she ran ahead of me. 'I won't fall,' she said. 'I'm too careful.'

She was right. I stood at the bottom of the wall and watched as she climbed. Every move of her hands and feet was carefully planned, and she never looked like she was in the slightest bit of danger.

'Come on, Lauren,' she called as she balanced on the ledge at the top of the wall. 'Hurry up. The weather is lovely up here.'

I didn't answer. I took a deep breath as I started to climb, clinging tightly on to every hand and foothold. At last I was sitting on the ledge beside Tilly.

'Isn't it so brilliant up here?' she said.

Again, I didn't answer. I'd never admit it to Tilly, but I'm really nervous about high places. I like to keep my feet firmly on the ground, and right now I felt very, very uncomfortable.

Tilly showed no sign of moving any time soon.

'I'm going down,' I said in the end. 'It's a bit cold up here.'

I scrambled down as best I could, and when I got to the bottom, I felt like kissing the solid ground under my feet. Tilly was beside me in a second.

'Come on,' she said. 'Let's go up again. I'll race you.'

I shook my head. 'You go. I'll wait over there on that bench.'

Tilly didn't argue and soon all I could see were the soles of her shoes as she made her way to the top again.

I sighed and went to sit on the bench. There were loads of people in the park, jogging and cycling and playing ball. The sun was still shining, and it was kind of peaceful watching everyone else being so energetic, while I was just sitting doing nothing.

A few minutes later, an old woman came and sat on the other end of the bench, placing her shopping basket on to the grass beside her.

What was she doing invading my space and spoiling my peace?

'Hello,' she said in a quiet voice.

I didn't answer. It wasn't totally rude of me. My parents always say I shouldn't talk to strangers. They'd be proud if they could see me being so obedient.

'Hello,' the old woman said again, a bit louder than before.

It seemed mean to ignore her a second time.

'Er, hello,' I said, trying not to sound too friendly.

Why couldn't she just go away?

The woman gave a small smile, like getting me to reply was a big achievement.

'Can I tell you something?'

Great!

She probably wanted to tell me some boring story about what life was like a thousand years ago when she was a little girl.

I didn't answer, but my small nod was enough to make her continue.

'I used to be crazy,' she said.

Double great!

I wasn't just talking to a stranger; I was talking to a crazy stranger.

And I wasn't reassured by her use of the words 'used to be'. Crazy was crazy, wasn't it? Only thing was – the woman didn't look crazy, she just looked old and tired and a bit sad.

Still, I wasn't taking any chances. I was edging further away on the bench when she spoke again.

'A long time ago, I used to imagine things – all kinds of things. For a while, I couldn't tell what was real, and what wasn't real.'

'That sounds awful,' I said, forgetting that I was trying not to be interested.

She nodded. 'It was awful.'

She stopped talking, and I began to hope that she'd got to the end of the story. Then she spoke again.

'Of course, crazy isn't a nice word. It's the word that the boys who shouted at me in the street used to use.'

'That's totally mean,' I said, feeling a sudden flash of anger on her behalf.

She sighed. 'They didn't understand. They were just little boys.'

I didn't know what to say. I was starting to feel very sorry for this woman, crazy or not.

She went on speaking in the same quiet voice. 'The doctors never used the word "crazy", though. They said I was mentally ill. Anyway, whatever you call it, it wasn't much fun. But the doctors cured me. They gave me pink tablets and blue tablets and white tablets, and in the end I got better.'

Now what was I supposed to say? Was I supposed to congratulate her?

A group of teenagers came and sat on the grass near the bench, making me feel a bit safer. If the old woman started any weird stuff, help would only be a few metres away.

The woman continued. 'I still have to take the white tablets – two in the morning and two in the evening. They don't taste very nice, but they work. And for the past ten years, everything has been perfect.'

She stopped talking and seemed to be waiting for me to say something.

'Er . . . I'm very happy for you,' I said in the end, wondering if it would be rude of me to leave now.

Tilly was on her way up the climbing wall for what must have been the tenth time, and didn't seem to care that I was discussing pink and blue and white tablets with a stranger.

'Only thing is,' said the woman suddenly, 'I think I might be going crazy again, and that means I'm going to have to dispose of my darling Sattie – even though I love him so dearly.'

Totally great! Just when I was starting to relax, she was talking of killing somebody – probably her husband.

Should I tell someone? Who should I tell? Would the police believe me? Was this my chance to make a difference? Could I save the intended murder victim?

All I needed was a bit more evidence.

'Er . . . who exactly is Sattie?' I asked.

The woman wiped away a tear from one of her faded blue eyes.

13

'Sattie isn't his real name, of course. His real name is Saturn. He's my cat.'

For a second I was relieved. If this woman had a husband, it looked like his life wasn't in any immediate danger. Then I realized that this wasn't totally good news. 'You're going to kill your cat?'

She shook her head crossly. 'What kind of a woman do you take me for? When I say I need to dispose of Saturn, I mean that he can't live with me any more. I need to find him a nice home.'

I was relieved again. 'But if you love him so much, why do you want to get rid of him?'

She didn't answer for a long time. Her eyes were half closed, and for a minute I thought she had dropped off to sleep.

Then she spoke quickly. 'Saturn belonged to an old man who used to live near me. He was a nice man, but he was very strange. He was crazier than I've ever been. Anyway, he died a few months ago and poor Saturn had no one else to take care of him. So I adopted him.'

I smiled at her. 'That was nice of you.'

She nodded sadly. 'I was glad of the company. And at first Saturn and I were very happy together.'

She stopped talking. I was interested now and wanted to hear what happened next.

'But?' I prompted.

I just knew that this was the kind of story where there had to be a 'but'.

'But lately, I've started to imagine things again. Strange things seem to be happening to me, but I know they can't possibly be true. And they always happen when Saturn is around. He seems to influence my mental state. And, much as I love him, I don't want to be sick again. That leaves me with no choice. He has to go.'

It all sounded a bit weird to me, but who was I to argue?

What did I know about mental illness and multi-coloured tablets and cats that make people think that strange things are happening?

The woman ended with a final sentence that was almost like a sigh. 'But where can poor Sattie go?'

Once again she seemed to be waiting for an answer.

Suddenly I had a brainwave.

'Why don't you send him to animal welfare?' I suggested. 'They came to our school once and gave us a talk. They love animals there. They find homes for stray cats and dogs.'

The old woman shook her head. 'I thought of that,' she said. 'But it's easy to find homes for kittens. Saturn is all grown up. And he's not . . . well, let's say he's not like other cats. Saturn is a very special cat and he needs someone very special to take care of him.'

I couldn't think of anything else to say to this.

Where was Tilly when I needed her?

Then the woman said, 'My name is Betsy.'

She was edging closer to me on the bench. I wasn't scared any more – just a bit embarrassed.

She leaned over and pointed at my charm bracelet. I held my breath.

Was she going to try to steal it? Was I going to have to wrestle with this old woman to save my all-time favourite piece of jewellery?

'That's very pretty,' she said.

I nodded, wondering how offended she'd be if I pulled my arm away.

Then she stretched out one skinny finger and touched the cat charm that Amy had given me for my last birthday.

'And I see you're a cat lover.'

I nodded again and wondered where this conversation was going.

'And you seem like a very sweet, kind little girl,' she said. 'Am I right?'

I smiled. This woman was totally weird, but let's face it, who doesn't like hearing good stuff about themselves?

'I suppose I'm not the worst girl in the world,' I said.

Betsy slowly got to her feet. 'That's settled then,' she said.

Hang on a minute. What's settled?

'No . . . I . . .' I began.

She patted my arm with her wrinkly old hand. 'He's very affectionate when you get to know him.

17

And he likes lots of cuddles. Brush his fur twice a
week – he likes that. And be kind to him. Please.'

She was walking away.

'No,' I called after her. 'You don't understand.
I'm not . . .'

She moved very quickly for such an old lady, and
while I was still talking, she had left the park and
was on the road leading towards town.

Just then Tilly was beside me. She threw herself
on to the bench in the space where Betsy had been
sitting only moments before.

'I see you made a new friend,' she said. 'Bet she's
not as good at climbing as I am.'

'She was the strangest woman, but I couldn't help
feeling sorry for her,' I began. And then I went on
to tell Tilly the whole story.

'That's totally weird,' she said when I was
finished. 'But look on the bright side – at least she
didn't actually try to give you her cat.'

'I suppose you're right,' I said. 'That would have
been totally, totally weird. Now if you've spent
enough time climbing your own miniature Mount

Everest, do you think we can get out of here? Mum will be starting to worry about us.'

She laughed, and we both stood up.

Then Tilly grabbed my arm. 'Er, Lauren, there's just one thing,' she said, pointing to the ground near the bench.

'What do you think could be inside that basket?'

 3

There was a long silence as Tilly and I looked at the basket that was on the grass just near the bench.

It was an innocent-enough-looking basket – the kind Little Red Riding Hood might have taken on her walk through the forest to see her grandmother. It was made of some kind of straw, and there was a pink and mauve flowery cloth covering whatever was inside. It wasn't a big basket, so I knew it couldn't contain a wolf or a tiger or anything totally scary like that. Still, though, something about it was making me very nervous.

'Open it,' said Tilly.

'No way,' I whispered. 'You open it, since you're so brave.'

'But it isn't mine,' she protested.

'It isn't mine, either,' I said. 'It's . . .'

I looked up to see if there was any trace of the strange old woman, but she had long since vanished.

'It's not really anything to do with us,' said Tilly after another long silence. 'We could just go home and leave it there.'

Could we really just walk away?

Before I could decide what to do, the flowery cloth moved slightly. Tilly shrieked and grabbed my arm. 'There's something alive in there,' she said.

'Clever of you to notice,' I said, trying not to sound as scared as I felt.

'It's probably just –'

Before I could finish my sentence, the flowery cloth moved again and a faint sound came from the basket. It was a weird sound – like whatever was in the basket had something caught in its throat.

'I'm out of here,' said Tilly, without moving.

I didn't move, either.

I *so* didn't want to look in the basket, but at the same time, I *had* to know what was in there.

'How about we look in together?' I suggested. 'On the count of three.'

Tilly nodded, and I began to count slowly.

'One . . . two . . . three.'

Again, neither of us moved.

We both giggled nervously.

Just then, the cloth stirred one more time. It moved slowly at first, and then with a sudden flurry that made Tilly and me jump, the cloth was flung aside and something was sitting up in the basket, staring at us.

There was a very, very long silence.

'It's a cat,' said Tilly helpfully.

She was right, it *was* a cat.

But it was nothing like any cat I'd ever seen before.

It had long white hair and huge pointy ears. Strangest of all, though, were its eyes. One eye was pure bright blue, while the other was a deep, dark green colour.

Round its neck was a narrow leather collar,

studded with shiny green and blue stones – exactly
matching its eyes.

Tilly was still squeezing my arm, but now she
relaxed her grip slightly so that it only hurt a lot,
instead of an awful, awful lot.

The cat was blinking its odd eyes. It yawned, and
then licked its lips with its long pink tongue.

'Omigod,' I said again. 'It's going to eat us.'

Tilly actually laughed.

How dare she laugh, when I was so scared that I
was actually thinking of racing to the top of the
climbing wall to get away from this thing?

'Don't be such a baby, Lauren,' she said. 'It's not
going to eat us. It's just a cat.'

'Well, it's a weird cat,' I muttered, as I took a step
away from it.

Tilly released my arm and took a step closer to
the creature.

'Hello, Saturn,' she said. 'Aren't you the cutest
little thing I've ever seen?'

Cute isn't the word I'd have used.

Freaky or weird were the ones that came to my

mind first. But then Saturn bent his head and rubbed it against Tilly's hand. He made a soft purring sound and, for one tiny second, he did seem . . . well, maybe not cute, but not quite as weird as before.

Seconds later, Saturn was being cuddled in Tilly's arms.

'He's adorable,' she said. 'And it doesn't look as if your new best friend Betsy is going to come back, so . . .'

I was fairly sure where this was leading, but I waited for her to finish.

'. . . can I keep him?'

'Weren't you listening, Tilly?' I protested. 'I told you the whole story. Betsy spent ages talking to me before she made up her mind. She said I was kind. She said I was the perfect person to take care of Saturn.'

'But you said he was weird. You don't want him.'

She was half right.

When Saturn was an alien creature in the basket, I didn't want him. But now that Tilly seemed so interested, I was afraid of losing something special. Suddenly I very much wanted to keep this cat.

I leaned over and stroked his head. His fur was soft and silky. He blinked and stared at me with his bright odd eyes. I had a sudden, strange feeling that he was checking me out.

'He's not weird,' I said quickly. 'He's beautiful. He just frightened me for a minute, the way he popped up so suddenly. That's all. I'm over it now. And I have to follow Betsy's wishes. I promised.'

'No, you didn't.'

'Well, I would have, if she hadn't rushed off like that. Anyway, I think that cat is mine.'

Tilly didn't answer at first. She rubbed Saturn's back and he rewarded her with a loud *miaow*.

She sighed. 'It wouldn't work, anyway,' she said. 'My dad's totally allergic to cats. There's no way I could ever have kept him.'

She held her hands out and gingerly I took the cat from her. He snuggled into my arms. I could feel his heart beating against my skin.

'Luckily my mum loves cats,' I said.

This was true. Mum loves normal cats. I wondered if she could find it in her heart to love this beautiful but strange, odd-eyed cat.

Tilly was still stroking Saturn's head. It was time for me to be generous.

'You can help me to feed and take care of him,' I said. 'And you can play with him whenever you come to my house. He can sort of belong to both of us.'

'Thanks, Lauren,' she said.

Then she hesitated. 'There's just one thing, though. Didn't the old woman say that strange things happen whenever Saturn is around?'

She was right. I had forgotten that.

Should we be afraid of this creature?

But then I looked around the park. The sun was still shining. People were still hanging out enjoying themselves. Everything was normal, just like it should be.

Saturn snuggled deeper into my arms. He gazed up at me with his wide, peculiar eyes.

How could a cat make strange things happen?

'Betsy clearly had a lot of issues,' I said in the end. 'She didn't know what she was talking about.'

Tilly nodded. 'I suppose you're right,' she said. 'Saturn is just a poor cat who has been abandoned by his owner. It's lucky you were here to take care of him.'

I stroked Saturn's soft, smooth fur. 'See, kitty,' I said. 'Today is your lucky day. Let's go home and you can live happily ever after with me.'

We put Saturn back into his basket and tucked the cloth round him to keep him warm. He popped his head up and looked very happy as Tilly and I took turns to carry him back to my place.

'You were gone for ages,' called Mum from the living room, as Tilly and I let ourselves in the front door. 'Did you get lost?'

I smiled to myself as I put Saturn's basket on the floor in the hallway.

'No, Mum,' I said, 'we didn't get lost. But you know how you said that you never get any presents?'

4

There's something I should make absolutely
clear right now.

I'm just an ordinary girl.

I'm not some freak who wears weird clothes and
smells of mouldy cabbage. I'm not the kid you
wouldn't want to sit next to at school.

I'm not the kind of girl who hangs around
park benches chatting to strange, sad old
ladies.

I'm certainly not the kind of girl who ends up
adopting cats from strange, sad old ladies.

Even though that's exactly what I did.

*

Tilly went on the Internet to research cats.

'Saturn's a Turkish Angora cat,' she said when she called round the next morning.

'Sounds fancy,' I said.

'It is. It's a real posh breed, and lots of them have odd eyes – it's like their speciality.'

I giggled. 'So Saturn is a designer cat.'

She nodded. 'He's probably worth a lot of money.'

That gave me a horrible thought. 'Do you think Betsy will change her mind and want him back?'

Tilly shook her head. 'Not the way you described it. Sounds like she didn't want any more to do with him. Ever.'

I stroked Saturn's silky fur. 'Don't worry, kitty,' I said. 'I won't be like Betsy. I'll love you forever, I promise.'

After the first day with my family, Saturn's odd eyes only looked a bit freaky.

After the second day, they hardly looked freaky at all.

On the third day, I looked out of my bedroom window and saw a cat with perfectly matched green eyes and I thought it looked totally weird. I even felt a little bit sorry for it.

That's the day I knew that Saturn had changed my way of looking at cats.

By this time, Saturn had become part of our family and none of us could imagine life without him.

We'd had cats in our family before, but Saturn was the cuddliest creature who had ever shared our house with us. He slept on my bed, and I often woke up to find him curled up in my arms. Mum pretended to be cross about this, but I knew she wasn't really. In a way, I think she might have been jealous.

Stephen, who's usually afraid of cats, (and almost everything else) was brave enough to stroke Saturn, and I heard Amy telling her best friend that our new pet is 'totally cool'.

'That cat loves us all so much,' said Mum one day as she sat down – and had to duck as Saturn launched himself at her from halfway across the room.

Dad just laughed. 'Cats only love themselves,' he said. 'Saturn's just looking for a nice warm pair of arms to cuddle him.'

Maybe Dad was right, but it really didn't matter. Even he loved Saturn, and Saturn seemed to love us, so everything was perfect.

One damp, horrible day, I was hanging around the house, feeling totally bored.

One of Amy's friends had joined a band, and she was playing their music at full blast. (She could lie on her bed for hours, listening, like it was actually good.)

Stephen was playing some pointless war game on the computer.

Mum was just putting a cake into the oven when I wandered into the kitchen for what felt like the fiftieth time. I used my finger to scrape some of the cake mixture from the inside of the bowl. It was chocolate cake, which is usually my favourite, but I couldn't make myself get excited about it.

'Where's Tilly today?' asked Mum.

'She's visiting her cousins. She's going to be gone for ages.'

'Why don't you clean out your bedroom?' suggested Mum. 'It hasn't been tidied properly for weeks.'

Didn't she think I felt bad enough already?

'It's OK, thanks,' I said. 'I'll just go hang out in the living room and play with Saturn. He's acting a bit strangely today.'

Mum smiled. 'It's probably just the damp weather. Would you like something to drink? There's some lemonade in the fridge.'

I nodded.

Mum gave me a full glass of lemonade, which I emptied in seconds.

'Thanks, Mum,' I said. 'But I'm still totally bored.'

Mum smiled again. 'Your life is too soft, young lady,' she said. 'What you need is a big dose of reality.'

I didn't feel like a lecture, so I put the glass into the dishwasher and went back into the living room. I picked up Saturn's brush and sat on the floor.

'Come on, Saturn,' I said. 'You haven't been brushed in days. What would Betsy say if she knew?'

Saturn saw the brush, jumped off the couch and ran towards me.

I smiled. 'That's a good boy,' I said. 'Sit there nicely and I'll make you the most beautiful cat in all of Ireland.'

Saturn blinked his eyes as I started to brush the long fur on his neck, next to his collar. It was kind of relaxing, running the brush through his silky coat, listening to his soft, satisfied purring.

Then suddenly Saturn's purr changed to a harsh growling sound. His body went tense and his eyes became wide and staring.

I put down the brush and stroked his head.

'Hey, Saturn,' I whispered. 'What's wrong?'

He didn't answer of course. He jumped into my arms and gazed at a patch of carpet near the window, like it was the most amazing thing he'd ever seen.

I followed Saturn's gaze across the room, but there was nothing unusual there – no mouse, no butterfly, not even a single lazy buzzing bluebottle.

Even through my fleece, I could feel Saturn's

claws pressing into my arms. He looked fierce and wild and a bit scary. I could see that he was ready to pounce. I wasn't very happy to be his springboard, but boy was I glad I wasn't his intended victim.

'It's OK, Saturn,' I said softly. 'There's nothing –'

Before I could finish, Saturn hissed loudly and then flung himself across the room like a sleek, white bullet.

He landed on the patch of carpet that he had been staring at, and seemed puzzled that it was just a plain, empty space.

I started to laugh. 'Silly Saturn,' I said. 'If you want to hunt, first you have to make sure that there's something there. Hunting is no fun without a target.'

Saturn looked at me with wide, staring eyes, and then he gave a small, strangled howl and leapt back into my arms, landing heavily.

'Hey, that hurt,' I said, as I struggled to catch my breath.

Saturn clung on to me with four rigid paws. He looked absolutely terrified. This didn't seem funny any more.

'It's OK,' I said, stroking his trembling head. 'There's nothing there. You don't have to –'

But I couldn't finish the sentence.

I felt suddenly dizzy and the room was spinning.

There was a strange whirring noise, like a helicopter revving up for take-off.

'Mum?' I tried to say, but the word didn't make it out of my mouth.

All of a sudden there was a white, blinding light.

I tried to hold Saturn, block my ears and cover my eyes, but discovered that two hands aren't quite enough to do all of these things.

And then everything went blank.

 5

At last the whirring noise stopped. I still felt slightly dizzy and my head hurt. Saturn was still in my arms, but he seemed to have relaxed a bit. (Or maybe I was just getting used to the feeling of his claws embedded in my skin.)

My eyes were tightly shut and I was too afraid to open them.

I wondered if there had been an earthquake, or a tornado or something else that belonged more in my geography book than in my living room.

Could an aeroplane have crashed into the roof of our house? (If an aeroplane crashed into your roof, would you still be sitting there wondering what had happened?)

I wriggled and tried to make myself feel comfortable. Why did the carpet suddenly feel so lumpy? How come I could feel cold air on my skin? How come Amy's music had gone quiet for the first time in weeks? How come I could hear birds singing, and smell grass and cows and other country stuff?

I opened my eyes.

'Omigod,' I whispered.

Instead of our nice brown and white stripy carpet, I was sitting on a big, dirty heap of straw.

Instead of our living room, I was in a small field, surrounded by crumbly stone walls.

How can a house just vanish?

I had absolutely no idea where I was or how I had got there. This was like some crazy dream – except I knew for sure that I was awake.

'Mum?' I called, not really expecting an answer.

'Mum?' I called again. 'This so isn't funny.'

Still there was no answer.

'Mum?' I called, feeling more confused than I ever had in my whole life.

The birds were still singing, and far away a cow mooed loudly.

I slowly got to my feet. My arms and legs hurt, like I'd been running a marathon or something.

This was *sooo* weird.

I put my hand into the pocket of my shorts and pulled out my phone. I switched it on and pressed the buttons to call my mum. I held the phone to my ear, but heard no sound. I looked at the screen and saw, NO NETWORK AVAILABLE.

Great!

What kind of loser place has no network available?

I shoved my phone back into my pocket and put Saturn down on the grass, where he began to sniff around, like nothing strange had happened.

I was starting to feel seriously scared. I don't generally hang around fields all that much – shopping centres and cinemas would be more my kind of thing. And this field was really starting to freak me out.

There was a gap in the stone wall and I walked

towards it. I was glad when Saturn trotted along beside me. I slipped through the gap and found myself on a rough, muddy road. Saturn turned left and I followed him, simply because I couldn't think of anything else to do.

I walked for ages and ages. Soon I was feeling sick and dizzy and lost and very, very sorry for myself.

Only minutes earlier I'd been sitting in my own living room in the middle of the city, and now I was in some weird country place with only a cat for company.

It just didn't make any sense.

This kind of thing isn't meant to happen in real life. Real life . . .!

I stopped walking and slapped my forehead.

I thought back carefully. When I complained about being bored, Mum had said I needed a dose of reality.

Did she mean reality TV?

I remembered a film I'd seen a few months earlier. It was all about a man who thought he was living a normal life, but it turned out to be one long reality TV show.

But would Mum enrol me in some weird TV show without telling me?

I had a funny feeling that she might. She's always going on about reality shows and how she'd love to take part in one. Once she even wrote away to a TV production company offering to take the whole family to a deserted island for two weeks. (Luckily they said no. They said we were too 'normal' – proving that they hadn't met Amy or Stephen.)

I held my breath. Was I going to walk round the next bend and see Mum sitting outside some old country house, milking a donkey or planting a spaghetti tree or doing whatever it is that people do in the country?

Would I be cross, or would I just be glad to see her?

I didn't want to be on a reality TV show, but right then it seemed like a better option than anything else I could think of.

I looked all around, wondering if there was a camera following me.

There was nothing of course – they'd never make it that obvious.

Then I suddenly ran over to a gap in the wall, hoping to surprise some unsuspecting TV person, who'd be all embarrassed at being discovered.

But all I could see was more grass, more walls and more fields, stretching for as far as I could see.

Very clever, I thought. *No expense spared. I must be a part of a very big production.*

But that still didn't make any sense.

In reality TV shows, the contestants always arrive at their new homes in helicopters and limos or at least in big, shiny jeeps with the number plates blacked out.

I hadn't done that, or at least I couldn't remember doing that.

Could I have bumped my head and lost my memory? Did I need to see a doctor?

Just then I licked my lips and tasted something sweet. I remembered the lemonade Mum had given me. Had it been drugged?

Would she drug her own daughter just to get on

TV? I wasn't sure I wanted to know the answer to that question.

I looked all around again, but nothing had changed.

I hoped it wasn't going to be one of those programmes where the contestants have to do tasks. There was no way I was eating worms or snails or eyeballs or gross stuff like that. There was no way I was climbing any high things, either. I didn't want millions of people laughing as they watched me tremble at the top of a tree, or halfway across a rope bridge.

OMIGOD!!

Millions of people!

I pulled my hair out of its ponytail and tied it up again, neater than before. I straightened my fleece and brushed some pieces of straw from my shorts.

If I was going to be on TV, it was important to look my best!

 6

Saturn had stopped in the middle of the road, but now he started walking again. Once again I followed him.

Then we turned a bend and I saw a small house at the side of the road. Saturn slipped into a field and vanished from view.

I didn't panic, as I'd suddenly had a wonderful thought. Could this be where my mum and dad were waiting?

I tried not to smile as I came closer. Maybe this was going to be a bit of fun.

I jumped as I suddenly noticed that there was a boy sitting on the wall at the side of the house. He looked about eleven years old. He was dressed in old-fashioned clothes. He had short, greasy hair and a dirty face.

Was he another contestant, or was he part of the production?

'Hello,' he said with a big smile. 'My name's Mikey Spillane. What's yours?'

'Lauren.'

He started to laugh. 'That's a strange name,' he said.

Like Mikey is such a cool name.

'And your clothes are strange too,' he added.

Like any normal boy would be seen dead in the dirty rags he was wearing.

But I wasn't getting involved in a row. This show could go on for weeks and I didn't want to get marked out as the troublesome girl who's hated by everyone.

So I sat on the wall next to 'Mikey', bit back all of my smart comments and waited to see what else he had to say for himself.

'What brings you here?' he said then.

Clearly he'd been rehearsing his lines. Did

everyone else get an advance information pack? If so, where was mine?

'What brings you here – to Ballyboher?' he said again.

I sniggered. Ballyboher! How do they think up those names?

Still, maybe I should play along for another little while.

'Oh, you know – this and that,' I said. 'What about you?'

He smiled proudly. 'I live here. All this land is mine. This is my farm.' As he spoke he waved his hand over the small field behind him.

Did they think I was totally gullible?

'*Your* farm?' I said. 'Aren't you a bit young to be running a farm?'

He looked hurt. 'I'm eleven and a half, and I do all the work around here.'

'What about your family?' I asked, forgetting for a second that I wasn't going to believe a word he said anyway.

'My mother died and my father went to Scotland

to look for a job, and Granny Bridget is too old to do farm work.'

'Aww, such a sad story,' I said. 'I'd cry, only I know it's all made up.'

Now he looked really, really hurt.

'Why would I make up a story like that?' he asked.

I had to hand it to him. The kid was a good little actor. But I was getting a bit fed up with all the pretence. If there were tasks to be done, I might as well get started.

I sighed. 'It's OK, Mikey, or whatever your real name is,' I said. 'I know what's going on. I know this is a reality show.'

Now he looked puzzled. 'I understand "reality",' he said, 'but what is a reality show? I've never heard of that.'

He wasn't fooling me, so why wouldn't he just give up?

How much were they paying this guy?

(Actually, now I came to think of it, how much were they going to pay me? There's this really cool touch-screen phone I've had my eye on for ages.)

'Mikey, I told you it's OK,' I insisted. 'So you can quit acting – even though you're very good at it. I know it's a reality show. I know this is all a set-up.'

'A set-up?'

'Yes,' I said, starting to feel angry. 'I know it's all a set-up for TV.'

Mikey looked at me with huge, innocent eyes.

'What's TV?' he asked.

And that's when I began to understand that I was in very, very big trouble.

Ten minutes later, I was still crying. Mikey put his hand into his pocket.

'You can have a loan of my hanky,' he said.

'Thanks,' I said, holding out my hand and then pulling it back quickly when I saw the filthy rag that Mikey seemed to think was a hanky.

The poor boy looked embarrassed, and I couldn't blame him. There he was, minding his own business, and a crazy girl shows up and starts talking like an idiot. Then he asks a perfectly harmless question and she starts to cry like a big, stupid baby.

47

I wiped my eyes and held back my sobs as best I could. Then I gave Mikey my fiercest stare.

'I'm going to ask you one question,' I said. 'And I need you to tell me the truth. It's very, very important. Do you understand?'

The poor boy looked totally confused.

'Why would I want to tell you lies?' he asked.

Because the truth might make me cry even more?

'Well, whatever,' I said. 'Just answer the question.'

He gave a small smile. 'Just ask me the question,' he said.

I took a deep breath.

'What year is it?'

Mikey started to laugh. 'That's it? That's your hard question? I'm not stupid, you know. I go to school at least three days every week.'

'Just answer the question,' I said, from between gritted teeth.

He gave a big sigh. 'If you don't know the year, then that makes you the stupid one, not me.'

'OK, so I'm stupid, I admit it. Just tell me the answer.'

'It's 1912.'

I put my hand over my mouth to stop myself from crying out.

Mikey had to be telling the truth. But how could that be the truth? How could it be 1912?

This was no reality TV show; this was something much worse.

This was reality.

Just then Saturn appeared through a hole in the wall. He stretched himself and then jumped into my arms. I hugged and kissed him like I hadn't seen him for years and years. (Which might have been true, when I thought about it properly.)

'What is that thing?' asked Mikey, sliding away from me on the grass.

I felt a sudden burst of anger. Saturn was my only link with my normal life and no one was going to insult him – not even this kind boy with the grubby hanky.

'It's not a thing,' I snapped. 'It's a cat. It's *my* cat.'

'That's a cat?'

'Of course it's a cat. His name is Saturn.'

'I've never seen a cat like that before. He's got hair like a girl and his eyes don't even match.'

Mikey was edging further away, looking a bit scared.

I cuddled Saturn again, clinging on to him like he could make this whole thing less scary. Saturn licked my hand with his warm, rough tongue, and I scratched behind his ears the way he loved.

Mikey was making a face. 'I can see that you love him, but he still looks strange to me.'

'OMIGOD,' I shrieked, making Saturn jump, and making Mikey reach for his so-called hanky again.

'What's wrong?' he asked.

I'd just remembered Betsy, the old woman from the park. She'd had to get rid of Saturn because, when he was around, she started imagining things. Suddenly I was fairly sure what kind of stuff she had been imagining – strange, going-back-in-time kind of things. The poor woman hadn't been ill at all. This cat really did make strange things happen.

I held Saturn up in front of my face and stared into his odd green and blue eyes. He stared back, almost like he could understand how upset I was. I could see myself reflected in his huge pupils.

'It's you, Saturn,' I said softly. 'You did this.'

Saturn didn't answer, of course, but if he had, I wouldn't have been the least bit surprised. I didn't think anything could surprise me now.

I shook Saturn gently. 'You got me here,' I said. 'So now bring me back home. Please. Joke's over.'

Saturn continued to stare at me in unblinking silence.

'I'm scared,' I whispered. 'I don't like this weird kind of stuff. I don't even like reading about this weird kind of stuff. Please just bring me back to where I belong.'

Saturn blinked once, then jumped from my arms. He went off to lie in a patch of sun at the side of the road. Without him, my arms felt empty and cold.

Mikey was edging closer to me, reminding me that he was there. I didn't care that he'd just heard me begging a cat to take me home – after all, he

51

thought I was crazy anyway, so what difference could this make?

'You never told me what you are doing here in Ballyboher,' he said.

And I was supposed to be able to answer that?

It's not like I wanted to be stuck in stupid Ballyboher.

I wanted to be back in my own house, lying on the couch, listening to Tilly telling one of her never-ending jokes. Or hearing Amy's friend's rubbish band singing their rubbish songs.

I wanted to hear Stephen screaming at the computer screen.

I wanted to hear my mum in the kitchen, rattling pots and pans and humming in the way that usually annoyed me so much.

I wanted to be bored again.

Mikey patted my back like I was a baby.

'It's all right, Lauren,' he said. 'You don't have to be scared. I'll look after you.'

And then I started to cry again.

7

Eventually I stopped crying. After all, how was that going to help me? It wasn't like I could cry myself a huge salty sea so that I could swim back to the future.

Saturn had settled down for a snooze. I felt a sudden urge to run over and curl up next to him. He could snuggle close to me, the way we both loved. I could shut my eyes and listen to the soft, grunting noises he makes when he dreams, and maybe convince myself that I was back home.

But what good would that do me?

Mikey was still sitting beside me, looking embarrassed.

'Where are you from, anyway?' he asked.

When are you from? would have been a better question, but how could the poor boy possibly have known that?

'I'm from Dublin,' I said.

'Wow,' he said. 'I've never been to Dublin. My father has, though.'

'So you know how to get there?'

He shrugged. 'Not exactly. But leave it to me. I'll find a way to get you back home.'

I smiled my thanks, but couldn't feel reassured.

Was my fate suddenly in the hands of a grubby, badly dressed eleven-year-old boy?

And even if this boy did somehow manage to get me to Dublin, what was I supposed to do when I got there? Sit in a field where my house wasn't yet built and hang around for a few decades waiting for my parents to be born?

And when they eventually were born, would I be older than them? Could I rock my mother's pram, and feed a bottle of warm milk to my baby father? Or show my great-grandad my phone and tell him that he'll have to wait eighty years before he gets to see another one?

This time-travel thing was far too complicated for me.

But getting to Dublin would at least be a start. If I sorted out the place, maybe the time would sort itself out on its own.

Suddenly I shivered. The shorts I was wearing were very suitable for August, but I had a funny feeling that it wasn't August any more.

'What month is it?' I asked.

Mikey must have been getting used to my weird questions because he answered without hesitation.

'April. Thursday, April the eleventh, if you want to be exact.'

I was stuck in the wrong century, so what did it matter if it was April or August? But even so, I could feel the tears beginning again. Was I going to cause the great Ballyboher flood of 1912?

Mikey patted my arm.

'I have an idea,' he said. 'I have to go on an errand to Queenstown this afternoon.'

'Queenstown?'

He laughed. 'Queenstown is a huge big town.'

If it was a huge big town, how come I'd never heard of it before?

'And you can get a train to Dublin from there,' he continued.

'Yesss!' I said. 'Can we go now?' I jumped up.

Mikey hesitated and looked back at the field behind him, which was half dug.

'I have to sow carrots first,' he said.

I felt sorry for him, but I felt sorry for me too. I didn't like being lost.

Maybe my parents already had an international search party out looking for me.

Maybe my face was already staring out of every newspaper in the country. (If it was, could I be sure they'd used a flattering photograph of me? If they'd used that gross one Dad took last Christmas, I would never *ever* speak to them again.)

'Please,' I said.

'All right,' he replied. 'I can do the carrots later.

Let's just go inside first and Granny Bridget will get us something to eat.'

Something to eat sounded good – after all, I hadn't eaten for almost a hundred years.

So I took a deep breath and followed Mikey into the tiny house.

We were in a small, dark room. There was a huge fire burning and beside it sat an ancient old lady who was knitting furiously.

'Granny, this is Lauren,' said Mikey. 'She's coming to Queenstown with me, but can we have some food first?'

The old woman nodded and put down her knitting. Then she came over to me and patted my hair and stroked my face. Her hand was thin and rough, and it felt a bit like I was being stroked by a chicken's claw.

'Er, hello . . . Mrs . . .' I began.

'You can call her Granny Bridget,' said Mikey. 'Everyone does.'

'Hello, Granny Bridget,' I said, and she smiled at me.

Mikey and I sat by the fire until my legs were warm again, and then I helped him to put cutlery on the table.

A few minutes later, Granny Bridget served up the food.

I sat down and she handed me a plate. There was a hunk of hard-looking bread and a greasy scrap of bacon about the size of a fifty-cent piece. Mikey gave me a cup of warm milk.

And even though I'm more a lasagne and pizza kind of girl, I dived into the food like it was the finest I had ever eaten.

When the meal was over, Mikey found some even staler bread, which he mixed up with a drop of milk in a small bowl.

'What's that for?' I asked, hoping it wasn't dessert.

'It's for your strange cat,' he said with a grin.

I followed him outside, wondering how I could explain that Saturn only ate a special kind of dried food that you had to buy at the vet's office.

Saturn came bounding over when he saw us, and I was amazed when he ate every scrap of the mushy mess. Clearly he understood that it didn't pay to be fussy when you were stuck in 1912.

I wondered if he'd been in 1912 before. Or if he had any idea what was going on. I wished he could talk, so he could tell me what he knew.

Shortly afterwards, Mikey picked up the empty bowl and we went back inside.

'Time to go,' he said.

'Er, how exactly are we travelling?' I asked, fairly sure that I wasn't going to like the answer.

Mikey looked at me like I was an idiot. 'In a horse and cart, of course. How else would we get there?'

Car, bus, train, motorbike, aeroplane, jet-ski, space shuttle?

'How else indeed?' I said glumly.

Mikey ignored me. 'Our neighbour Paddy is lending me his horse and cart.'

Mikey picked up a towel and wiped his face. Then he licked his hands and used them to flatten his hair.

'Now,' he said. 'I'm ready.'

Then he looked at me.

'What?' I asked.

'It's . . . it's . . . it's your clothes.'

I looked down at my shorts and T-shirt and fleece.

I knew what he meant. I was fairly sure that my clothes weren't exactly the height of 1912 fashion – and while I like to be adventurous, being almost a hundred years ahead of the current trends was a bit extreme, even for me.

'People will think you are very strange if you go to Queenstown dressed like that.'

He was right, but what was I supposed to do? Grab Granny Bridget's wool and needles and knit myself a suit? Weave myself a dress from a bundle of old straw?

Mikey smiled shyly. 'All of my mother's clothes are still here. She was thin like you, so I know they would fit. You can borrow something, if you want.'

I hesitated. Could Mikey really part with something that had once belonged to his mother? Did I really want to wear a dead woman's clothes?

But I knew he was right.

My trip was going to be difficult enough, without everyone staring at me like I was a total freak.

So I let Mikey lead me up a shaky ladder to a dark attic.

'Er . . . Mikey,' I said, finding it easier to speak in the darkness. 'Earlier, when you said about your mother dying and stuff, I wasn't very sympathetic. I'm sorry . . . you see . . . I –'

'It's all right,' he said. 'You were upset.'

I nodded. 'I know, but that's no excuse, and my friend Tilly – her mother died too, so I know how hard it is.'

'Tell your friend that I'm sorry for her troubles,' he said.

'Sure I will,' I said – *if I ever see her again.*

Then Mikey opened a big trunk and pulled out a faded brown dress. He held it up proudly.

'This is the one. This was my mother's Sunday best,' he said.

I didn't answer. The poor woman must have really looked forward to Sundays.

Not.

Mikey patted my arm awkwardly. 'I would like you to have it,' he said. 'And my mother was a very generous woman. I think she would have wished you to have it too.'

It didn't seem fair to argue with a dead woman's wishes, so I nodded my head. 'Thank you,' was all I could think of saying, though it didn't feel like enough.

Then Mikey tucked the dress under his arm and we both slid down the ladder.

In the kitchen I unzipped my fleece.

Mikey gasped. 'What is that?'

'What?'

He pointed to the zip, feeling the thick plastic teeth.

I laughed. 'Don't tell me you've never seen a zip before.'

'I've never seen a zip before,' he said solemnly.

I took off my fleece and tried to show Mikey how the zip worked.

'That's magic,' he sighed. 'Real live magic.'

I put the dress on over my T-shirt and shorts. It fitted perfectly, coming right down to the ground and covering my runners. The dress was made of thick brown material. It had long sleeves and a high, ruffled neck. It was probably the ugliest dress I had ever worn, and I was glad there wasn't a mirror anywhere nearby. I didn't want to see how awful I looked.

'You look very nice, Lauren,' said Mikey shyly. 'A real fancy lady.'

I turned away so he couldn't see how selfish and mean his comment made me feel.

8

Ten minutes later we'd said our goodbyes to Granny Bridget, and we were trotting along a narrow country road in Mikey's neighbour's horse and cart.

Mikey was grinning. 'It's good to travel in style,' he said. 'We're like the king and queen of Munster.'

I didn't answer. My teeth were rattling in my head, and even though I was sitting on my fleece, I felt sure that I was already black and blue from bouncing up and down on the hard bench.

Saturn was curled up on some old blankets on the back of the cart, looking very sorry for himself.

'Granny Bridget's really nice,' I said, to distract myself from the pain. 'How old is she?'

Mikey shrugged. 'I don't know. I don't think she even knows. But I know she was alive during the famine.'

I gulped. 'You mean like *the* famine? The one in the history books? When the potatoes all went bad? Your granny was alive then?'

He nodded.

I wished that I'd asked the old lady a few questions, so that the next time I had to do a history project, I could do it about the famine and it would be so authentic I'd get top marks.

And then I gave up on that thought.

Maybe I'd never get back to my real life, never again be in my school doing projects. Maybe I'd stay stuck in the past forever, becoming my own personal real-life history project.

'Do you have brothers and sisters?' asked Mikey, shaking me out of my sad dreams.

I nodded. 'One of each. They're both really, really annoying.'

He sighed. 'I wish I had brothers and sisters.'

Suddenly I felt sorry for him again. Amy and

Stephen might be a pain, but we do have fun sometimes. And, back in my real life, I had a mum who was alive and a dad who lived in the same country as me. Poor Mikey had none of that.

Mikey continued. 'There's a boy in my class and he has seven brothers and four sisters. When I go past his house, I can hear them all talking together. They sound so happy.'

Seven brothers and four sisters sounded like a nightmare to me, but what did I know?

'When I grow up,' he went on. 'I'm going to get married and have a whole house full of children, all laughing and playing together all day long. I won't ever get cross with them because I'll be so glad that they are there. A big family is the thing I want most in the whole world.'

'You go for it,' I said.

He giggled. 'You know, you say very strange things. Sometimes it's almost as if you speak a different language to me.'

I smiled. 'You want to hear more strange talk?'

He nodded.

Then I said really fast, 'Computer, DVD, spaceship, Nintendo, satnav, microwave, tumble-drier, laptop, remote control, interactive whiteboard, plasma screen . . .'

I stopped for breath and Mikey laughed and clapped his hands.

'You are so good at making up words,' he said. 'I wish I could do that.'

I grinned. 'You could, but it would take a long time to learn – probably most of a hundred years.'

Then we were quiet for a while. It was hard to know what to say. Tilly and I never have enough time to say all the things we want, but none of the things that Tilly and I talk about were suitable topics of conversation in 1912.

Have you seen the latest phone? Anything good on TV tonight? My laptop's broken?

Mikey pulled on the reins, slowing the horse.

'You should rest, Lauren,' he said. 'You've got a long journey ahead of you.'

Ha! He had no idea how true those words were.

The cart stopped completely. Mikey leaned back

and rearranged the blankets on the back of the cart, making a softish place for me to rest.

'Giddy-up,' he said then, and the cart lurched forward, making me tumble down backwards on to the heap of blankets.

'Sorry,' said Mikey, but I could see from the shaking of his shoulders that he was laughing.

I laughed too, glad that this serious boy had room for a sense of humour.

'I'll wake you when we get there,' he said.

As I tried to make myself comfortable on the blankets, Saturn slid over beside me.

'I don't like being here,' I whispered as he snuggled close. 'But I'm glad you're with me.'

Saturn blinked once, and then closed his eyes, shutting me out and making me feel suddenly lonely.

So I closed my eyes too, and soon the sway of the cart lulled me into a deep, dreamless sleep.

It felt like only minutes later that Mikey was shaking my arm gently.

'We're here, Lauren,' he said. 'This is Queenstown.'

I rubbed my eyes and climbed down from the cart. Saturn sat up, stretched, and then jumped into my arms.

Mikey climbed down from the cart too. He seemed shy.

'The railway station is that way,' he said, pointing. 'Ask for directions if you can't find it. Have you got money for the train?'

'Yes,' I lied.

I knew Mikey had no money to give me and I didn't want to make him feel bad. When the time came I'd think of something.

'Here,' he said, holding a small, paper-wrapped package towards me. 'Take this for the journey.'

I knew it was the sandwich Granny Bridget had made for him. I didn't want to take it and deprive him of his only food. And I hoped I'd never be hungry enough to want to eat the greasy lump of bacon fat she'd put into the sandwich.

So I smiled. 'Thanks, but no thanks. I'll get food on the train.'

Mikey was the kindest, sweetest boy I have ever known, (in any time-zone). Even though we'd only known each other for a few hours, I felt closer to him than I felt to some people I'd known for years.

I desperately wanted to give him something – to try, in some small way, to repay all his kindness to me.I felt my shorts pockets through the brown dress. In one pocket I could feel my phone, which wasn't much use to Mikey, or anyone else in 1912.

I racked my brains. If I couldn't give Mikey a thing, surely there was some information I could give him that would help him sometime in the future?

Suddenly I remembered something that had happened in a film I'd seen years earlier. It was a time-travel film (and I'd seen it back when I believed that time travel was just an impossible, crazy fantasy).

'Hey, Mikey,' I said. 'Listen carefully and remember this. Spain are going to win the World Cup in 2010. If you go to the betting shop and back Spain early, you can make heaps of money.'

I thought I was being very clever, but Mikey just looked puzzled. 'The World Cup for what? What's a betting shop? I don't understand what you are saying,' he said.

'You don't have to understand,' I said. 'Just remember. World Cup. Spain. 2010. Write it down and keep it safe. One day it will make sense, I promise you.'

'OK,' he said. 'Whatever.'

I smiled at his use of the new words I had taught him, but my smile faded quickly as I calculated in my head. By the time 2010 came around, Mikey would be well over a hundred years old. What were the chances of him still being alive? Would he remember an encounter with a very strange girl in funny clothes who had appeared out of nowhere, one sunny April day in 1912? If he did remember, would he think it was just a foolish boyhood daydream?

'I'd better get going,' I said.

I *soooo* wanted to hug Mikey, but I had already figured out that in 1912, boys and girls didn't hug until they were practically married. So I held out my hand and he took it in his, and we shook firmly, like we were making a deal.

Then Saturn and I set off to find the train station.

I'd never felt so alone in my whole life.

For a minute, I thought about going to the police – after all, even in 1912 it must have been their job to take care of lost children.

But what were they supposed to do? Were they going to say – *Oh, yes, our time-travel machine is just about to leave – it's being fuelled up as we speak. Hop on board and we'll have you back with your family in no time?*

No chance.

They'd just listen to my story and then fling me into some grim home for deranged orphans, and I'd never be seen again.

If I was going to get home, I was going to have to do it all on my own.

9

The town was very busy with people pushing and shoving and hurrying. No one paid any attention to me as I walked along in my ugly brown dress with my cat in my arms. At home, everyone stares at Saturn, but here no one seemed to notice him at all – maybe they had too many other things on their minds.

'Do you know where the railway –' I began to ask a man, but he just pushed past me, without a glance.

'Thanks for nothing,' I said, and walked on.

Soon I came to a big dock area where there were even more crowds. Lots of people were hugging each other and crying. Many people were standing next to huge stacks of bags and suitcases.

There were some small boats tied up along the side of the dock, and far out across the water I could see a huge ship.

Suddenly Saturn wriggled out of my arms and ran towards the edge of the dock. 'Hey, come back,' I called. 'We're looking for a train, not a boat. And besides, cats are supposed to be afraid of water.'

As usual, Saturn ignored my calls and made his way through the crowds. I followed, terrified of losing sight of him.

'How did I ever get stuck with such a useless cat?' I muttered as I ran. 'Why couldn't Betsy have given me a dog – a nice, obedient dog?'

I didn't mean that, though – not really. Since this whole mess had started, Saturn hadn't done a lot to help me, but in the crazy world I had stumbled into, he was my only hope. If I was ever to get home again, I knew Saturn was going to have something to do with it. And besides, if I didn't have Saturn to cuddle when I felt low, how was I ever going to cope at all?

I pushed my way past a group of young boys, and

saw Saturn. He glanced backwards, almost as if he wanted to be sure that I was following him. He was almost within my reach, but as I stretched out my arms to grab him, I stumbled on my long dress and fell to the ground. I lay there for a second, stunned and scared. I could feel a trickle of blood on my knee.

Then I heard a gentle voice in my ear.

'You poor little girl. Please allow me to help you.'

I opened my eyes to see a kind-faced man with a huge grey beard. He looked like Santa Claus's grandad. I took the hand he was holding towards me and got to my feet.

'There's a bench over there,' he said. 'You should go and sit down and catch your breath.'

I shook my head. This was no time for luxuries like sitting on benches and catching my breath.

'I'm fine. Thanks very much,' I called over my shoulder as I raced off in the direction Saturn had taken. I could feel my heart thumping wildly as I got to the very edge of the dock.

Saturn was nowhere to be seen.

I put my face in my hands and tried to hold back the wave of terror that was starting to wash over me. This was all much too scary.

I wanted Saturn in my arms. I wanted to be safe in my own house.

I wanted Mum and Dad and Tilly.

All I wanted was not to be right there, right then.

Just as the first hot tears were filling my eyes, I heard a distinctive, hoarse *miaow*. I turned round to see a small girl standing in a line, a little bit away from me. She had a pale, round face and tiny, dark eyes. She had long, blonde curly hair and was wearing a silk dress with a big lace collar. She looked a lot like the china doll my granny gave me for my seventh birthday. In her arms was a hairy white bundle.

'Saturn,' I whispered with relief.

I ran towards them. 'Hey,' I said. 'Sorry, but that's my cat.'

The girl stuck her tongue out at me and shoved Saturn into the basket she was carrying. Saturn blinked at me once with his green and blue eyes and then curled up, as if a nap in this little girl's basket was exactly what he had been dreaming of for years. The girl stuck her tongue out at me a second time and covered Saturn with a pink fluffy blanket.

She *sooo* wasn't getting away with that.

As I reached to put my hand into the basket, the woman standing next to the girl turned round. She looked at me like I smelled bad, which might have been true since it was nearly a hundred years since I'd had a good hot shower.

'Go away, you nasty little thief,' she said in an icy voice. 'Or I'll call the police.'

'But she's got my cat,' I said.

'I've never heard such an outrageous lie. I don't see any cat,' said the woman haughtily. 'Now come along, Ernestine, before you catch something nasty from that dirty girl.'

Ernestine gave me a sly smile. 'Yes, Mother,' she said.

Before I could say anything else, the woman showed some papers to a man. He looked at them and then handed them back to her.

'There you go, Mrs Jones,' he said. 'Have a safe journey.'

Then Ernestine and her mother made their way along a wide, wooden walkway, leading towards one of the small boats. They sat on a bench on the deck of the boat, and the girl turned back and gazed at me with a small smile lurking at the edges of her pale, thin lips.

I raced towards the walkway, but the man stepped forward to stop me.

'Not so quick,' he said. 'Let's see your ticket.'

'I don't have a ticket. I don't want to go anywhere. Well, actually, I do want to go somewhere, but not anywhere the boat can take me. I just need to talk to that little girl over there – just for one second. She's got something that belongs to me.'

Ernestine quickly turned her back towards me and snuggled closer to her mother.

The sailor looked at their fancy clothes and then at my shabby brown dress.

'A likely story, you young ragamuffin,' he said. 'Now run along before I call the police.'

That was the second time in a few minutes that I'd been threatened with the police. I was turning into a one-girl crime wave. Tilly would laugh when I told her – if I ever saw Tilly again, or got the chance to tell her anything.

I could see two sailors beginning to unwind the rope that was holding the boat tied to the dock. I could hear the grinding noise of the engine, and then the boat pulled off from the shore.

I stood and watched in horror. Second by second, the boat was getting further and further away. It was taking Saturn, and with him, any chance I had of getting back to my future.

Suddenly it was all too frightening for me. Tears poured down my cheeks and I began to sob loudly.

'Dear, dear me. You really are having a bad day, aren't you?'

I turned to see the kind old man who had helped me when I fell.

'May I do anything at all to assist you?' he asked.

I pointed out to sea. 'I have to get to that boat. My ca–' I stopped suddenly. He seemed like a very kind man, but would he help me if I told him I had lost my cat?

I couldn't take any chances.

'My mother,' I corrected myself. 'My mother has gone on that boat. I have to get to her. It's very important.'

'Now, now,' he said. 'Surely your mother wouldn't leave without you?'

I had to think quickly.

'Of course she wouldn't. But you see, she thinks I'm on the boat. And I was on it for a minute. But then I ran off for a second to say goodbye to my friend. That's when you saw me – when I fell down. But when I came back, the boat was gone.'

The man stared at me through his small, gold-rimmed glasses.

'You wouldn't tell me a lie, would you, young lady?'

I looked as innocent as I could and crossed my fingers behind my back.

'No, sir. I swear it. I would never tell you a lie.'

If this wasn't so very, very important.

He smiled as he took me by the arm.

'Well, I think I might be able to help you,' he said. 'As you know already, that small boat is going out to the big boat. And just along the quayside here, there's another boat that's going to do exactly the same thing. So if you will allow me to help you to get on the second boat, you'll be back with your mother before she even realizes that you are missing.'

This was getting more complicated than I had hoped for. I really wasn't sure that I wanted to go on either the big boat or the little boat. But I had to get Saturn back and I couldn't see how I was going to manage this by staying on dry land.

So I smiled at the man. 'Thank you, sir,' I said. 'That's very kind of you.'

The man led me along the dock to where there was another boat, just like the first. There was a line of people waiting their turn to board. Luckily a different sailor was checking tickets, and he almost bowed as my finely dressed new friend went up to him.

'What can I do for you, sir?' he asked.

'This little lady has managed to get separated from her mother, who has left on the other tender.'

The ticket checker looked a bit doubtful, but my friend persisted.

'I cannot stand by and see this poor girl stranded without her mother.' His voice was gentle, but he sounded like a man who was used to being obeyed.

The ticket checker still didn't move and I could see that my new friend was getting impatient.

'You must have a list of passengers so that you can check,' he said. 'Tell the gentleman your name, young lady.'

I gulped. Why did there always have to be a catch?

And then I had a sudden flash of inspiration.

'Ernestine,' I said. 'My name is Ernestine Jones.'

The ticket checker ran a dirty finger along a list of names.

'There's a Mrs Jones and her daughter Ernestine.'

I grinned. 'Yup. That's me. I'm Ernestine Jones.'

'But you and your mother are meant to be on the other boat. And you don't have a ticket.'

I knew he was weakening, so I dived into the argument.

'That's the whole point,' I said. 'You see, Mrs . . . I mean, my mother has accidentally gone without me. And she has my ticket in her backpa– I mean, her purse. She is going to be frightfully worried.'

I was very convincing – so convincing that I almost believed my own story. I took a deep breath and started to cry real tears.

The old man patted me on the head. 'There, there,' he said kindly.

He glared at the ticket checker. 'This young lady needs to be reunited with her mother without further delay. If you don't allow her to board, I shall have no alternative than to speak to your superiors.'

The ticket checker reluctantly stood back to allow me to pass on to the boat. I raced along the walkway and stood on the deck.

I turned to wave my thanks to my new best friend, but he had already vanished.

10

We seemed to travel for miles, and soon Queenstown was only a hazy blur in the distance. The rocking of the boat was starting to make me feel a bit sick, so I sat on a bench and closed my eyes. I tried to imagine what I'd do when I saw Saturn again – I was torn between kissing him and strangling him.

After a while, the gasps of the other passengers disturbed my thoughts. I opened my eyes.

'OMIGOD,' I whispered to no one in particular.

We were next to the biggest ship I had ever, ever seen. I felt dizzy as I gazed up at the huge expanse of steel. It was like Tilly's favourite climbing wall – multiplied by a hundred.

The small boat pulled up beside a door cut into the side of the ship, and everyone climbed through.

In the corridor, there was a man in a white uniform, telling people where to go. He looked at my untidy hair and Mikey's mother's shabby dress.

'Third class, I presume?' he said, pointing along the corridor.

I looked the way he was pointing and saw lots of shabbily dressed people just like me. When I looked in the other direction, I could see a group of people who looked more like Mrs Jones and Ernestine.

'I can see my mother over there,' I said, and before the man could argue, I walked quickly towards a group of well-dressed strangers. Then I walked past them and continued my search.

I was totally lost as I made my way through corridors leading off corridors in what seemed like a gigantic maze.

After ages I found myself out in the open air. Passengers lined the decks, leaning over the railings and waving at the distant shoreline.

'Lauren,' shouted a familiar voice.

I turned and saw Mikey running towards me.

'What on earth are you doing here?' I asked.

He held my fleece towards me. 'You left this on the cart,' he said. 'And since it's got the special zip thing on it, I knew it was important to you. I searched everywhere and at last I saw you leaving on the small boat. I shouted, but you didn't hear me – so I knew I had to follow you.'

'And how did you get here?'

He grinned. 'I met a man from Ballyboher who was coming out here to sell lace to the rich passengers. He gave me a spin.'

Mikey had gone to all that trouble just to give me back an ancient old fleece that I'd never liked a whole lot anyway.

Suddenly I didn't care that it was 1912. I reached out and gave him a huge hug.

Mikey looked embarrassed.

'You know, Lauren,' he said. 'You seem a bit confused sometimes, so I have to tell you, this is a ship, not a train.'

I smiled. The poor boy must have thought I was a total idiot.

'I know,' I said.

'So come back with me to the shore and I'll show you the way to the railway station.'

I shook my head. 'I can't. Saturn's somewhere on this ship and I have to find him.'

'He's just a cat.'

Yeah, just a cat who's my only hope of getting back to the twenty-first century, where I belong.

'It's kind of hard to explain,' I said. 'But I can't leave without him.'

'I'm very sorry, but I can't wait for you,' he said. 'My friend told me to hurry – the ship is leaving soon.'

'Here,' I said suddenly, handing him my fleece. 'You keep this. You can give it to your first little girl.'

He took the fleece and tentatively played with the zip. Then he touched the logo.

'I couldn't.'

I smiled. 'It's not such a big deal. They're quite common where I come from.'

Mikey stroked the fleece like it was the most precious thing he had ever owned.

'Thank you,' he said.

'You're welcome.'

'Will you write to me when you get home – to let me know that you arrived safely?' he asked.

I smiled a vague smile. Who knew if I'd ever get home again? And if I did, even though our postal service is good, I couldn't expect it to work miracles.

'I'll do my best,' I said. 'But don't you worry about me. I'll be fine.'

Suddenly there was a series of loud whistles. Some people near us started to cheer and a few leaned on their friends and cried. I could feel the floor rumbling under my feet as the engines revved up.

A woman near me was waving madly at the shore. 'Goodbye, Ireland,' she called.

I gulped. I didn't like the sound of this.

'Where exactly are we going?' I asked.

The woman looked at me like I was a total idiot.

'America, of course. We're off to New York.'

I gulped again, louder this time.

I *sooo* didn't like being stuck in Ireland in 1912 and I *sooo sooo sooo* didn't want to be stuck in New York in 1912. (After all, none of the shops I liked would be open until the next century.) I had to find Saturn and get back to shore.

I grabbed the arm of a sailor who was walking past.

'My friend and I aren't meant to be here,' I said. 'This is all a terrible mistake. Don't let the ship start yet. I need to find Sa– I mean, I need to find someone important and then we need to get off.'

The sailor laughed, but not unkindly. 'There's no getting off now, young lady. It's too late for that. Next stop New York. You just relax and enjoy the trip.'

Easy for him to say. He wasn't stuck in the wrong time, and rapidly heading towards the wrong place too.

Beside me, Mikey had gone pale.

'I can't go to New York,' he whispered. 'Granny Bridget needs me. I haven't sown the carrots yet – or the potatoes. And Paddy will go mad if I don't bring his cart back.'

'So what are you going to do? You heard what the sailor said.'

'I'll get back to my friend's boat.'

'But what if he's left already?'

'Then I'll have to jump off this ship.'

'You can't swim to shore, it's miles away.'

He waved towards the water.

'There's loads of small boats out there. One of them will pick me up. I'll be fine. I'm hardy.'

'Don't do anything stupid,' I said. 'Don't –'

Before I could finish the sentence, he'd started to run. I watched him dart behind a group of people, towards a small door.

He stopped and pulled the fleece on over his shirt. 'Thanks, Lauren,' he called. 'My daughter will be the best-dressed girl in Ballyboher.'

Then he ducked through the door and was gone.

I stood on the deck, fighting back the tears.

Maybe I should have gone with him. But if Mikey's friend had already left, I'd have been too afraid to jump into the water. (Tilly's a great swimmer, but I can only do two lengths of our local pool without stopping for a rest.)

And without Saturn . . .

Before I could finish the thought, there was a huge rush of smoke and the sound of the engines changed.

'We're off,' shouted a man beside me. 'At last we're off.'

It took me ages to push through the crowds, to get to the back of the ship. There were lots of boats bobbing in our wake. There was no sign of a small swimmer dressed in a bright pink fleece.

Was Mikey safe on one of the boats, laughing as he demonstrated the zip to his friend from Ballyboher?

Or was he . . .?

'Mikey,' I whispered.

What if he was in the water? What if he had put himself in danger, and all because of me?

I ran up to the nearest sailor.

'We have to stop,' I said. 'I think my friend might be in the water.'

The sailor seemed worried at first. He pulled a whistle from his pocket and stared out at the churning expanse of water.

'Point to where you saw your friend last,' he said.

I turned round and pointed to the doorway where I'd last seen Mikey.

'Over there,' I said. 'He went through there.'

Now the sailor looked more angry than worried. He put the whistle back into his pocket.

'Did you see him in the water?'

I shook my head.

'Did you see him fall off the ship?'

I shook my head again. 'No. But –'

The sailor pushed past me. 'I have work to do,' he said. 'And I have no time for hysterical girls like you.'

'Please,' I whispered.

Suddenly the man softened. He climbed on the railing and took another good long look at the ocean.

'There's no one there,' he said. 'I'm sure your friend is fine. You'll both laugh over this later on.'

I wasn't totally convinced, but what could I do?

So I turned away and continued to search for the stupid cat who was the only one who could get me out of this stupid, stupid mess.

Much later, when I felt that I had walked hundreds of miles, I found Ernestine on one of the decks. She was still carrying her basket, but I could see that it no longer contained a cat. She was crying like someone had poked their fingers in her eyes.

'My kitty runned away,' she wailed to no one in particular. 'My kitty runned away and I can't find him.'

'Shush, Ernestine,' said her mother crossly. 'It's "ran away", not "runned away". And you know there was no kitty there anyway. That nasty, scruffy girl just made it up. Now go and play with your dollies.'

That made Ernestine wail even louder. Real tears poured down her round, pale cheeks. In different circumstances, I might have felt sorry for her, but not now. This whole mess was all her fault. If she hadn't taken Saturn, I wouldn't be stuck on this stupid ship. If it weren't for Ernestine, I could have been halfway to Dublin by now.

So I ran past her and continued my search.

Shortly afterwards, I found myself on a deserted deck, near the back of the ship.

'Saturn,' I called for the hundredth time. 'Where are you?'

I was just turning to leave, when I heard a familiar *miaow* from over my head. I looked up to see Saturn staring down at me from the inside of a lifeboat.

I scrambled on to a railing, reached up and took Saturn into my arms. I hugged him tightly and he licked my face.

'You silly kitty,' I said. 'Look at all the trouble you've got us into. All I want is to go home. I don't know how you got us both here, but you'd better start to figure out how we're going to get back. I don't like boats, I don't want to go to New York and I am *so* fed up of being stuck in 1912.'

Saturn just licked his lips and gave another *miaow*.

'You know you can be really annoying sometimes,' I said, but once again he ignored me.

'Well, see if I care,' I said. 'You can stay up here for as long as you like. At least Ernestine won't be able to find you.'

Almost as if he understood me, Saturn wriggled out of my arms and on to the seat of the lifeboat. He stretched and then curled himself up, out of sight underneath the lifeboat covers. I thought about slipping in next to him, but just then my stomach gave a huge grumble and I remembered that I hadn't eaten for hours.

Suddenly I was very sorry that I had refused Mikey's bacon sandwich.

'You stay there, Saturn,' I said, as I climbed down from the railings. 'And be careful. I'm not sure if cats are allowed on ships, so it's better if no one sees you. I'm going to find myself something to eat. I'll get something nice for you too. I'll bring you a special treat. I'll be back in a –'

Then my words stopped and my hunger vanished, as an ice-cold, shivery chill ran up and down my spine. My legs went weak and I slumped down to the ground.

I looked at the back of the lifeboat, rubbed my eyes and then looked again.

Nothing had changed.

The sea was still dark blue and wavy. The lifeboat was still big and white and shiny. And the letters on the lifeboat still spelled out

LIFEBOAT No. 7
RMS TITANIC.

 **11**

Later, I was still sitting on the hard wooden boards of the deck. It wasn't especially cold, but I was shaking all over. This was the scariest thing that had ever, ever happened to me. I knew that crying wasn't going to help me now, but I couldn't stop.

Getting stuck in the past was bad enough. Getting stuck on a boat bound for New York in the past was bad enough. Getting stuck on the *Titanic* was the worst thing ever.

I thought of all the boats that had sailed in all the time zones of all the world. There must have been thousands, if not millions of them.

So how come I'd got stuck on the only one that I

knew for sure was going to hit an iceberg and sink to the bottom of the icy sea?

Soon my throat was sore and my head hurt. I wasn't crying any more, but I couldn't hold back the horrible, hiccupy sobs. The sleeves of Mikey's mother's dress were soaked with my tears.

Then I heard footsteps. I looked up to see a sailor approaching. I scrambled to my feet and raced towards him.

'We've got to turn back,' I cried. 'It's an emergency!'

The sailor laughed. 'An emergency, is it? Did you forget to kiss your boyfriend goodbye?'

I shook my head angrily. This was no time for jokes – especially for ones as pathetic as that.

'It's a *real* emergency. This ship is going to sink!'

The sailor laughed even louder.

'Don't be silly,' he said. 'Everyone knows that the *Titanic* is unsinkable.'

'Please!' I begged. 'You've got to listen to me. I can't explain how I know, but I know for sure that this ship is going to sink. You have to do something before it's too late.'

Then the sailor stopped laughing. He leaned forward and looked closely at my clothes. All of a sudden, I knew that Mikey's mother's best Sunday dress wasn't going to impress him.

'Aha,' he said. 'I wasn't born yesterday. I know why you're making up this tall tale. You thought I might get distracted and not notice that you shouldn't be here. You know well that this deck is reserved for first-class passengers. Now come along with me and don't make a fuss. I'll bring you back to where you belong. You'll be happier with your own kind.'

He was a huge man and I knew there was no point in resisting as he took my arm and half led, half dragged me along the deck.

Soon we came to a gate. Still holding me with one hand, the sailor used the other hand to take a key from his pocket. He unlocked the gate and pushed me gently inside.

'Be a good girl and stay with your own people

from now on,' he said. 'Things are easier for everyone that way.'

Then he locked the gate again and returned the way he had come.

I was still clinging on to the gate when I heard a quiet voice behind me.

'Must be lovely in First Class.'

I turned to see a girl who looked like she might be about my age.

'Are you feeling all right?' she asked, looking at my red eyes.

I'm perfectly fine, thank you – except for the fact that this ship is going to sink very soon.

'It's just the wind,' I said. 'It's so strong that it's bringing tears to my eyes.'

Why did I bother lying? We were on the *Titanic*, after all, and I knew what was going to happen next.

She held out her hand. 'I'm Mary,' she said. 'What's your name?'

At first I didn't answer. I wasn't sure I had time for making friends. I had a few thousand people to save from an icy, watery death.

100

But then I figured that if I was going to save this ship, I might need some help, so I reached out and took her hand in mine.

'I'm Lauren,' I said, as we shook hands politely.

Mary smiled at me. I wondered how friendly we would have to be before I got around to mentioning casually that the ship we were on was going to sink soon.

Then my stomach rumbled and I realized that I wasn't going to be able to save anyone if I died of hunger first.

So I smiled back at her. 'Any idea where we can get something to eat?' I asked.

'Of course,' she said. 'I was just on my way to the dining room. It's very grand. I'll show you, if you like.'

I followed Mary and soon we were standing in a huge room. It didn't look very grand to me, but what did I know? I was only an accidental tourist from another time and place. Crowds of noisy people were seated round large tables.

'Are you on your own?' asked Mary.

I wasn't sure how to answer this. I knew that in

the present I'm too young to fly on my own, but would I have been allowed on the *Titanic* on my own?

For the millionth time since I'd been in 1912, I wished that, just for one minute, I could get to a computer to Google something.

Mary was waiting for an answer.

'Er, I'm with my mum and dad,' I said quickly.

She looked around the room. 'Where are they?'

Good question.

'Er . . . Mum has a very bad cough, so she's going to stay in her cabin for a while. Dad is taking care of her.'

Mary took my arm. 'Come and sit with my family so,' she said, leading me across the room.

We stopped at one of the big tables. 'Mammy, this is Lauren,' said Mary.

Mary's mother had a gentle, tired face. She smiled as the small baby she was holding wriggled on her lap.

'Hello, Lauren,' she said. 'It's nice to meet you. This is Baba.'

I was just thinking what a strange name that was for a baby, when Mary explained.

'We haven't given him a real name yet. We're going to do that when we get to America. It'll be a new name for Baba and a new beginning for us all.'

The baby gurgled at me and then broke into a huge, gummy smile. I thought he was the sweetest baby I had ever seen.

Mary and I sat down, and for a while no one said much, as big plates of food arrived. Beef and gravy and soggy carrots wouldn't usually excite me, but I was so hungry it seemed like a feast. I tried not to look too greedy as I stuffed my face. Then, when I hoped no one was watching, I pushed a few scraps of food into the pocket of my dress, to give to Saturn.

When the food was finished, Mary told her mother the story about my imaginary mother with her imaginary cough, and my imaginary kind father who was taking care of her.

Mary's mother patted my hand. 'I have some cough medicine in my cabin,' she said. 'Mary can bring it to you later.'

Then Mary turned to me. 'My daddy is already in America,' she said. 'He went there last year. He's got a job and a place for us to live. It's called an apartment and it's got two rooms – imagine that! When I see my daddy, I'm going to give him the biggest hug he's ever had. He's going to be so happy to see little Baba – he's never seen him before. And he's going to choose a name for him too.'

Mary's big sparkly eyes and her happy smile were starting to make me feel sick. I couldn't bear to hear her talking about her plans for a wonderful new life in America – plans that might soon be coming to a very sad, very watery end.

'Daddy wrote us a letter. It came just before we left.'

As Mary said this, she pulled a very tattered piece of paper from her pocket. She flattened it out and started to read what her father had written.

'"I've already asked the foreman for the day off, so I'll be able to meet you all. When the *Titanic* pulls into New York, I'll be there waiting on the dock. On that day, I'll be the proudest and happiest man in all of America.'''

Mary refolded the letter and put it carefully back into her pocket.

I could feel the blood rushing from my face. The poor man had a long wait ahead of him. The *Titanic* was never going to dock in New York or anywhere else.

Would Mary ever hug her father again? Would her father ever see his sweet little baby boy? Would poor little Baba die without a name?

I had to do something.

I jumped up from the table.

'Er . . . excuse me,' I said. 'I have to go to see how my mother is doing.'

'I'll walk to your cabin with you,' said Mary, and before I could object, she had jumped to her feet and was waiting for me to lead her to my imaginary cabin.

12

I walked as slowly as I could, with Mary walking equally slowly beside me. I tried to make it look like I had a place to go, and like I knew how to get there. Mary didn't seem to be paying much attention to where we were going anyway – she was still talking about how much she was looking forward to seeing her father again.

Mary was a really nice girl, but I wondered how I was going to get away from her.

And I wondered what I was going to do when I did get away from her.

Suddenly I stopped walking and turned to face her. I knew I couldn't tell her the truth about the *Titanic*. She'd never believe me. And even if she did believe me, what on earth could she do about it anyway?

But I had to talk to someone, and it wasn't like I had a hundred friends all lined up waiting to give me advice.

'Mary, what would you do if you could go back in time and change the past?' I asked.

She wrinkled her forehead. 'What do you mean?'

'Like, if you knew something really bad was going to happen, would you try to stop it?'

'What kind of really bad thing?'

I racked my brains trying to think of something to illustrate my point. The problem was, none of the disasters I could think of had actually happened yet.

'Like the famine,' I said in the end, thinking of Granny Bridget. 'What would you do if you went back in time to just before the famine? Would you warn the people about the blight? Would you tell them not to plant potatoes that year?'

'But they only had potatoes,' she said. 'If they didn't plant them, they would have starved anyway. What else could they do?'

107

I slapped my forehead. She was right, of course. It wasn't like the poor people could have gone to the garden centre and bought a few courgette or asparagus plants instead.

'Bad example,' I said.

'So give me another one,' she said, smiling. 'I like this game.'

I felt like crying. How could I make her see that this wasn't a game, without frightening the life out of her?

'I can't think of another example right now. I haven't got time.'

'But we've got lots and lots of time.'

No, we don't. Not when we're racing towards an iceberg that has our name on it.

'Examples are stupid anyway,' I said. 'Just tell me – would you warn people, if you could go back in time and if you knew something bad was going to happen to them?'

'That's a lot of ifs,' said Mary.

'I know, but what would you do?'

She thought for ages – like she had all the time in the world.

Then she shook her head slowly. 'No,' she said. 'If it has already happened, then that's the way it was meant to be. It would be wrong to change it. Wouldn't it?'

I didn't answer. Mary sounded so wise. But then she thought I was talking about some vague historical might-have-been stuff.

Would she have been so wise if she knew I was talking about stuff that was going to happen to her?

Very soon.

'My cabin is just up here,' I said. 'Thanks for walking with me.'

She smiled. 'You're welcome,' she said, as she turned and walked back the way we had come.

As soon as I got round the next corner, I stopped walking. I sat on the floor and leaned my back against the wall. I put my head into my hands as I tried to think straight.

Tilly had got the *Titanic* DVD for Christmas, and for months it had been our favourite film. We'd watched it at least five times.

Each time I'd seen it, though, I'd been looking at Kate Winslet's pretty dresses and fancy hairstyles.

I'd gazed at Leonardo DiCaprio and hoped that, despite what I knew, one time he was going to drag himself on to a passing deckchair and be saved, so that he and Kate could live happily ever after.

But what good was all that stuff going to do me? Why hadn't I paid attention to the bits that might help me now?

Like how much time did I have left?

I knew that the ship didn't sink on the first night, but after that I had no idea. Was the ship going to sink tomorrow night, or did I have a few more days left to come up with a plan?

Tilly would know that kind of thing, but how could I ask her? She wasn't even born yet – her granny wasn't even born yet!

Granny!

I smiled to myself as I remembered one wet Sunday afternoon a few months earlier. I was watching *Titanic* with my granny, who is very old and very religious.

When the ship crashed into the iceberg she just shook her head, sighed and said, 'Little did they know.'

'Little did they know what?' I remembered asking her.

'When they were saying their prayers that Sunday morning, little did they know that they'd be going to meet their maker that evening.'

Good old Granny.

The ship was going to have its date with the iceberg on Sunday night. Mikey had told me that this was Thursday, so I had three whole days to come up with a plan.

But then I had another problem. Even if I could figure out a way to save the *Titanic*, was it the right thing to do?

Maybe Mary was right. Maybe it was wrong to mess with the past. Would saving all those lives change the course of history? Would it make things better or worse?

Maybe there was someone really evil on board who was supposed to die. If I interfered and saved his life, maybe he'd go on to invent some horrible bomb that would wipe out everyone on earth. And it would all be my fault!

Or maybe there was someone who would go on to be a dangerous driver. Maybe he'd go back to Ireland and knock down my great-grandmother. And then I'd never get to be born, and I'd never get to save the *Titanic* anyway.

I sighed. It was all much too complicated for me.

How could I hope to change something that I couldn't even begin to understand? Then I thought of Mary and how hopeful she was for her future in America.

I thought of her kind mother, who right now was probably measuring out medicine to give to my imaginary sick mother. I thought of Baba with his chubby fists and his gummy smile, and of Mary's father waiting in New York for the ship that was never going to arrive.

I thought of myself too – only twelve and with my whole life in front of me.

And I knew I had to do something.

13

I walked until my feet were sore. Most of the time I was totally lost and walking in circles. Every time I came to a gate that seemed to lead to the First-Class area, it was firmly locked.

Just when I was about to give up, I came to a corridor that was narrower than the others. A small sign on the wall said – STAFF ONLY.

I ignored the sign and walked along the corridor until I came to a single grey door. I pushed the door open and found myself in a storeroom. There were shelves from floor to ceiling, stacked high with sheets and towels.

One shelf was labelled – FIRST-CLASS TOWELS. I picked up a bright white towel and rested my cheek

against it. It was the softest thing I had ever felt —
like a cloud ought to feel. For one second, I thought
of making myself a bed from a heap of these soft,
cosy towels. I could curl myself up and drift off to
sleep. I could dream happy dreams and forget all
my troubles . . . until the icy water started to flow in.

The thought of the cold water pushed away all
thoughts of sleep. I put the towel under my arm
and looked around.

There was another door on the opposite side of
the room. I pushed this door open and couldn't
resist a small smile. I was on a much larger, fancier
corridor, and I knew at once that I had made it to
the First-Class section.

After much more walking, I found myself up on
deck. I put my hand into my pocket and felt the
scraps of food I'd saved for Saturn. I wasn't feeling
especially warm towards Saturn right then, but I
figured that I'd better feed him. He hadn't been a
whole lot of help so far, but if he died of starvation
he'd be even more useless.

I found lifeboat number seven and stood

underneath it, waiting for a very, very old couple to walk very, very slowly past. As soon as the coast was clear, I whispered as loudly as I dared, 'Saturn, are you still in there?'

I was rewarded with a small *miaow*, and a second later Saturn was peeping over the side of the lifeboat.

'You don't deserve it, but I've brought you some food,' I said, as I climbed up on to a railing.

I put the food on to the ledge where Saturn was sitting. He sniffed at it for a few minutes.

'Ha,' I said. 'Stop pretending to be so fussy. You ate every scrap of food that Mikey gave you.'

At the mention of Mikey's name, Saturn looked up at me. I wondered what was going on inside his head. Did the word 'Mikey' make him think of the kind boy we'd known, or did it just make him think of bread scraps mashed up with milk?

Anyway, whatever he was thinking, Saturn licked his lips and then began to gobble up the food.

As soon as he had finished eating, Saturn purred loudly and jumped into my arms. I couldn't resist hugging him tightly. I buried my face in his soft fur.

'I'm so scared, Saturn,' I whispered. 'I know you're the one who got me into this whole mess, but maybe it isn't your fault. I suppose you can't help being some weird, time-travelling cat, can you?'

Saturn purred again and licked my face.

I hugged him for a long time. His warm body was comforting and the beating of his heart next to mine made me feel the tiniest bit better.

After a while, I gave Saturn one last hug and lifted him back into the lifeboat. I unrolled the towel I had 'borrowed' from the laundry room and used it to make a soft bed.

'There, Saturn,' I said. 'Now you'll be all warm and comfy. You just stay here and have a nice sleep. I've got something very important to do. When I get a chance, I'll come back and let you know how I got on.'

Then I jumped down from the railing and set off on my quest.

Much later I found myself leaning over another railing and gazing down into what looked like the control tower of the ship. Inside were five men in uniform.

It didn't take me long to decide that the man with the beard was the captain. He had the fanciest hat, medals on his jacket and the most stripes on his sleeves. (And besides, he looked exactly like the captain in the film.) I watched him for a while, trying to decide what to do next.

While I was still making up my mind, the glass door opened and the man with the beard came out.

'Goodnight, captain,' called one of the others, and I smiled to myself. Even when your life is in danger, it's nice to be right.

The captain opened a gate in the railings and walked towards me. I had no time to plan what to say, but I couldn't let him go right past me. I might not get another chance.

I cleared my throat and tried not to notice the shaking in my voice as I spoke.

'Er . . . excuse me, captain,' I said.

He stopped walking and looked at me. He didn't

seem to notice that I wasn't dressed like a First-Class passenger.

'Well, good evening, young lady,' he said in a kind voice. 'And what can I do for you?'

I tried to think of what to say next, but was distracted by the thought that the captain looked exactly like the guy on the fish fingers packet.

For one second, I thought of home, and dinner with Mum and Dad and Amy and Stephen. There would be three fish fingers each and a big pile of baked beans.

Then I pushed that thought from my head. If I didn't do something quickly, I might never get to eat another fish finger.

(I don't even like fish fingers all that much, but the thought of never eating another one was just too sad.)

'Er . . . captain, can I speak to you for a minute?' I said. 'It's very, very, very important.'

The captain smiled at me. 'If it's that important, then I insist that you speak to me. Now what is it that you need to say?'

I thought hard. My next words were going to be very significant– for me and for thousands of other people. These were probably going to be the most significant words I had ever spoken.

I took a deep breath and began. 'I know you're going to think I'm crazy, but I'm not, I promise. It's just that . . . well . . . I know for sure that on Sunday night, this ship is going to hit an iceberg. And then it's going to sink, and –'

The captain put his hand up to stop me.

'Now, now,' he said. 'Enough of that nonsense. That's not going to happen. This is the *Titanic*. They don't call this ship unsinkable for nothing. It's been specially designed. Even if it did hit an iceberg, it still wouldn't sink.'

I struggled to remember the boring bits of the film – the bits with all the charts and diagrams, the bits Tilly and I usually fast-forwarded through.

'I know they thought the *Titanic* was unsinkable,' I said. 'I remember the kind engineer guy in the nice black suit was explaining it all to Kate Winslet . . .'

'Who on earth is Kate Winslet?'

I shook my head. 'You wouldn't know her, but anyway, I know this ship has all these special underwater section thingies.'

'Compartments?'

'Yes, that's it. Thanks. I know it has all these underwater compartments. But the iceberg is going to be massive and it's going to make a huge big hole. A few of the compartments are going to be damaged. I'm afraid I can't remember how many . . .'

'You can't remember something that hasn't happened yet?'

I hesitated. 'It's very complicated. But anyway, no one had thought of more than one or two compartments being damaged. But that's what's going to happen, so this ship is going to sink, and loads and loads of people are going to die, and . . .'

I stopped talking and started to cry.

The captain patted me on the head.

'Now, now,' he said. 'A little girl like you couldn't begin to understand the details, but trust me, the best designers in the world worked on this ship. It is absolutely unsinkable. Now you stop worrying your pretty little head and go back to your family.'

I'd love to, but no one in my family has been born yet.

'You *have* to believe me!' I said. 'I know for sure that it's going to happen.'

He smiled. 'How could you possibly know what is going to happen in the future?'

Because it's not my future. Because for me this is the ancient past! I've read the history books and watched the movie – done everything except buy the T-shirt.

'I just know,' I said lamely. 'I can't explain how, but I just know.'

The captain started to walk away, but I grabbed his arm.

'Please listen to me,' I said. 'Tell the driver to go slowly. Tell him to watch out extra-carefully for icebergs – especially on Sunday night. Tell him . . .'

The captain pulled his arm free. He looked a bit impatient now.

'I'm a very busy man,' he said. 'I have a ship to

run and I don't have time for this. Be a good girl and go back to your family, like I told you before. Stay with them and enjoy your trip. In a few days this ship will arrive in New York, and think how silly you will feel then. You'll know that you've been making a big fuss about nothing. Now, goodnight, my dear, and please stop fretting.'

He walked away.

I thought about following him, but I knew it wouldn't have made any difference.

His soft whistling made it clear what the captain thought of my story. He had decided that I was a silly, nervous child, and nothing I could say was going to make him change his mind.

Why couldn't I have had the *Titanic* DVD in my pocket when I got whisked back in time? And a fully charged portable DVD player.

Would the captain have listened to me if I could have shown him the movie, or would he just have thought it was all some crazy, futuristic notion, dreamed up by some weird kid in a shabby brown dress?

It didn't matter anyway. All I had in my pocket was my mobile phone that didn't have a signal.

I was hopeless and helpless.

Suddenly I wanted to be with Mary.

If this was going to be one of my last nights ever, I wanted to spend it among friends.

 # 14

I made a quick detour to hug Saturn goodnight.
He opened his blue eye when I stroked him.

'It didn't work,' I whispered. 'I did my best, but
the captain didn't believe me.'

Saturn didn't look surprised. (But then, he never
looks surprised. He always just looks mysterious.
Sometimes I wonder if he practises that look in the
mirror when I'm not watching.)

I wrapped the soft towel round him. 'Now,' I
whispered, 'you be a good cat and don't move. That
way, you'll be cosy and warm for the whole night,
and I'll come and see you in the morning.'

Saturn wriggled until he was comfortable and
then closed his eye.

'Goodnight,' I whispered, and then I made my way back to the Third-Class section.

I found Mary in the big dining hall.

'I've been looking everywhere for you, Lauren,' she said. 'I've got the cough medicine for your mother.'

She held a small brown bottle towards me. I felt embarrassed. I wasn't an expert on 1912 finances, but Mary and her mother didn't look like rich people. They probably couldn't spare this medicine.

Then I realized that, whatever happened to them in the next few nights, this medicine wasn't going to be a whole lot of good to them.

A private lifeboat would have helped. Or a rescue helicopter.

But this sticky brown bottle was going to be no use at all.

So I took the medicine from Mary and tried to look grateful.

'Thanks, Mary,' I said. 'I'll go and give it to my mother, and I'll meet you back here.'

Minutes later, I was back with Mary.

'That was quick,' she said.

That's because all I had to do was dash round the corner and shove the bottle into the nearest bin.

'My mother says to say thank you,' I said, feeling guilty about the lie. 'She said she feels better already.'

Mary smiled.

Suddenly I yawned. It had been a very long day and I was ready for bed – if only I had a bed.

'I think it's going to be hard for me to sleep with my mother coughing so much,' I said.

'I thought you said she was feeling better after taking the medicine,' said Mary.

'Oh, she is,' I said. 'But she was very bad before, and now she's not quite so bad, but she's still coughing a lot.'

Mary smiled happily. 'There are two spare bunks in my cabin,' she said. 'You would be welcome to sleep with us.'

I felt like hugging her. 'That's totally great,' I said. 'I love sleepovers.'

'Sleepovers?' said Mary, with a puzzled expression on her face.

'You know – when you go and sleep in your friend's house?'

Mary still looked puzzled. 'Why?'

So you can watch DVDs and check out your favourite websites and listen to music and make popcorn.

'So . . .' I didn't know how to finish.

Then Mary gave a sudden smile. 'I slept in my cousin Julia's house the night Baba was born. Uncle Denis played the fiddle all night long, and Julia and I danced until our feet were sore.'

I smiled. 'Yeah, that's the kind of thing I'm talking about. That sounds exactly like one of my sleepovers.'

Then I couldn't hold back a huge yawn.

'I'm a bit tired,' I said. 'Will we go to bed now?'

'Don't you need to tell your family where you are?'

She was right. I *sooo* needed to tell my family where I was.

But they weren't in a cabin round the corner. They were miles and years away, and I had no idea how to reach them.

'Oh, it's OK,' I said. 'I told them I might find somewhere else to sleep. They won't be worried.'

127

Mary looked doubtful. 'If you're sure,' she said.

I tried to smile. 'Sure, I'm sure. Now can we go?'

Mary's cabin was small. It had two sets of bunk beds, a tiny sink and nothing else. There was a loud throbbing sound from the ship's engines.

Mary's mother and the baby were already asleep in one of the bottom bunks. Baba was curled up in his mother's arms, with one chubby hand resting on her cheek.

Mary and I climbed into the top bunks.

Still wearing Mikey's mother's dress, I slipped under the thin blankets and made myself as comfortable as I could on the hard, narrow bed.

Mary and I whispered together in the darkness. It was like being on the weirdest sleepover ever.

I remembered the last sleepover Tilly and I had. We had both laughed so much, we'd almost made ourselves sick.

Where was Tilly now? Was she worried about me? Was I ever going to see her again? How long would it be before she made a new best friend?

Soon Mary gave a big yawn and turned to face

the wall. When I was sure she was asleep, I pulled my phone from my pocket and switched it on. There was only one bar of battery left.

I flicked through my old text messages. There were lots from Tilly. There was one from Dad, with a vaguely funny joke that he thought was totally hilarious. There was one from Mum, sent one afternoon when I'd been at Tilly's house. *Dinner's ready. Time to come home.*

'Oh, Mum,' I whispered to myself. 'I wish I could come home. I miss you all so much.'

I carefully typed out my reply. *Sorry, Mum. On the Titanic. Home ASAP.*

I pressed Send and smiled sadly to myself when the inevitable *Sending failed* message popped up. Then the battery died and the screen went black.

Soon hot, silent tears were pouring down my cheeks. I was in a room with some of the kindest people I had ever met, and still I felt lonelier than I ever had in my whole life.

15

I woke to see Mary sitting up in the bunk opposite mine. She grinned when she saw that I was awake.

'Good morning, Lauren,' she said. 'Aren't we so lucky to be waking up here on this big, exciting ship?'

Er . . . no.

'They call it the Ship of Dreams, you know.'

She wouldn't have said that if she knew what I knew. Ship of Nightmares would have been a much better name.

I stretched and sat up. 'Do you know where the showers are?'

'Showers?'

'Er, I mean the baths.'

'You want a bath?'

I nodded.

'But why?'

Because I shower every morning.

Mary's mother joined the conversation. 'There is one bath for Third-Class women,' she said. 'It's on the next deck. But we don't plan to use it. We all had baths before we left home on Wednesday. We'll be grand until we get to New York.'

Clearly they had different ideas of hygiene than I was used to. I had a funny feeling that the one bathroom wouldn't be equipped with fancy shampoo and conditioner and bath oils. So I waited my turn and washed myself as best I could at the tiny sink.

After breakfast, Mary helped her mother with the baby, and I sneaked off to feed Saturn. He was still curled up in his towel, looking like a very unusual, odd-eyed baby. I fed him and talked to him for a while. Then he curled up for another sleep.

'Well, you're a great help. Not,' I muttered as I climbed back down to the deck.

When I got back, Mary was waiting for me.

'Let's explore,' she said.

I went along with her, even though I already knew every inch of the Third-Class area.

I showed Mary the storeroom I had found.

She stroked the soft towels and the crisp linen sheets. 'When I grow up, I'm going to have sheets and towels like this,' she said.

I felt like crying. There was a real danger that this girl was never going to grow up.

'Look,' I said, pointing. 'This door leads to the First-Class area.'

Mary's eyes opened wide, like I'd just shown her the door to Paradise.

'Let's go there now,' I said.

Mary shook her head with a worried look on her face. You'd think I'd suggested robbing a bank.

'No,' she said. 'I wouldn't dare. They're all fancy people up there.'

I didn't feel like arguing with my new best friend. So instead, we borrowed two blankets, and then we went and found ourselves a quiet place on one of the

Third-Class decks. We sat down, and wrapped ourselves up to protect ourselves from the strong wind.

'Being here with you is so nice, Lauren,' said Mary.

I didn't answer. Sitting on the *Titanic* had never been top of the list of things I'd been hoping for in my life.

'You know, Lauren is the prettiest name,' said Mary then. 'I've never heard of it before. If I ever have a little girl, I'm going to call her Lauren. Then I'll always remember you.'

Mary's long curly hair blew around in the strong wind. Her eyes sparkled and her thin face became alive when she talked of her dreams of the future.

'I'm going to go to school in America,' she said. 'Daddy has it all arranged. And when I finish school, I'm going to work in a hat shop.'

I thought back to my only trip to America. All I could remember were shops selling tracksuits and hoodies and designer handbags.

'I don't think there's much of a market for hats in America,' I said, forgetting for a moment that this was 1912.

Mary shook her head.

'You're wrong. A lady is never fully dressed without a hat,' she said primly. 'And I'm going to design my own hats. I'm going to trim them with lace and feathers and pearls and I'm going to be the most famous hat-maker in all the land.'

I smiled, not trusting myself to speak.

'What about you,' she said. 'What do you plan for the future?'

How could I answer that?

If something didn't happen soon, I wasn't going to have much of a future to plan.

'I'm just going to chillax and see what happens.'

She laughed. 'You use the strangest words sometimes.'

I smiled. 'That's what Mikey said.'

'Who's Mikey?'

'Mikey was my very good friend,' I said.

'And where is he now?'

'I very much hope that he's at home in Ballyboher, where he lives with his granny.'

'And why wouldn't he be there?'

I sighed. 'It's a bit complicated.'

It was true. Everything in 1912 seemed to be complicated. There's a lot to be said for staying in the time and place where you belong.

Why couldn't I be at home, where my biggest problem was trying to decide what top to wear or what flavour ice cream to buy?

'I hope you'll still be my friend when we get to America,' said Mary. 'Please say you will.'

I wanted to answer. But what could I possibly have said?

It's complicated?

After lunch, Mary took my arm.

'Come with me,' she said. 'There are some people I'd like you to meet.'

Usually I like meeting new people, but right then the only people I was interested in were ones who were good at making lifeboats.

But still, I followed Mary down a corridor to a cabin. It was like the one I'd shared with her and her family, but this was even smaller, with just one set of bunk beds. Sitting on the lower bunk were a man, a woman and a little girl of about four years old. All three were thin and pale.

'They're very poor,' said Mary. 'And I think they are sick.'

I was wondering if it was rude to say this in front of them, when she continued. 'They don't speak English.'

'Er . . . so why exactly are we here?'

'I met them yesterday,' said Mary. 'Before I met you. And I brought the little girl, Magda, for a walk. The fresh air is good for her, and it gave the parents a chance to get some rest. If they still look sick when we get to America, they won't be allowed to stay.'

Mary reached out her arms and the little girl scrambled into them. She hugged Magda, and the girl hugged back, without smiling.

Mary held up one finger to the parents. 'One hour,' she said. 'I'll be back in one hour.'

The parents smiled gratefully, and we left, closing the door behind us.

'Let's go up on deck,' said Mary. 'The sea air will bring roses to Magda's cheeks.'

I got some more blankets and we found a spot on deck. For ages, Mary played with Magda. She sang to her, recited rhymes and tickled her, but Magda never once smiled. She just stared solemnly at Mary with her huge brown eyes.

Mary's patience seemed endless. It was nice watching how gentle she was with Magda, but after a while I started to worry about Saturn.

'I need to go check on my parents,' I said. 'See you in the dining room later?'

Mary nodded and I set off for First Class once again.

16

I fed Saturn and then lay beside him in the lifeboat.

'Take me home,' I said.

Saturn blinked.

'Take me home, please.'

Another blink.

'Pretty please?'

One more blink.

'Please, Saturn. Just tell me what to do and I'll do it,' I wailed. 'I know you know how to bring me back. Is there a magic word? Is it Abracadabra? Rumpelstiltskin? Muggle-wuggle? Open Sesame? Home Sesame? Sesame Street?'

Saturn licked my face once. Then he curled up and went to sleep.

'You're totally useless,' I said to the sleeping bundle of white fur. 'If you don't do something soon, you're going to find yourself having the biggest sleep of your life. And don't come crying to me when that happens because it will already be much too late.'

I climbed down and walked aimlessly along the decks, trying to work out what to do next.

If Saturn wasn't going to bring me home, my only hope was to stop the ship from sinking. And how was I supposed to do that?

I'd already tried telling a sailor and the captain, and neither of them had believed me. If I kept on talking about the ship sinking, the people in charge might decide that I was a dangerous troublemaker. They might lock me up below decks, like they did to Leonardo DiCaprio in the film.

And if the ship started to go down, I *sooo* didn't want to be in the basement, chained to a pipe.

I walked for ages and ages. On one of the decks, I saw Ernestine. She was sitting on a bench, talking to someone. I tiptoed closer and saw that she was

139

alone and talking to her dolls, who were all lined up in a row beside her. She was pointing to each one in turn.

'You're beautiful, you're beautiful, you're beautiful,' she said as she made her way along the row of dolls. Then she came to the last doll. 'You're not beautiful, Esmerelda, and I don't love you any more,' she said. 'You're too ugly.'

I smiled to myself. As far as I could see, all the dolls were a bit ugly, with their stiff hair, their staring eyes and their bright red cheeks.

Just then, a door opened. I ducked behind a pillar as Ernestine's mother leaned out through the doorway.

'Come along, Ernestine,' she said. 'Time to come inside.'

'Coming,' replied Ernestine. She picked up each doll, kissed it and laid it carefully in her basket. Then she got to the last doll. 'Not you, ugly-face Esmerelda. I don't want you any more,' she said.

Then she flounced off, leaving one doll behind her on the bench. As soon as the coast was clear, I walked over to the bench. The abandoned doll was lying face down on the seat. I picked it up and looked at it. Now that I could see her properly, I noticed that she was kind of cute, with twinkly eyes and a cheeky smile. On her forehead, there was a long, fine crack, probably the reason Ernestine had rejected her.

'Hm,' I said to myself, tucking the doll under my arm. 'You might not be perfect, but I think I know someone who will find it in her heart to love you. I'll have to think of a new name for you, though. You're getting a new life, so you need a new name.'

I found Mary in her cabin. She followed me into the corridor.

'Look,' I said, holding up the doll.

Mary touched the doll's stiff curly hair and felt her hard fingers. 'She's beautiful,' she sighed. 'Where did you get her?'

I hesitated. 'My granny gave her to me a long time ago,' I said in the end. 'But I've just decided that I'm too big for dolls.'

Mary's eyes widened, and I realized that for all

her serious, grown-up ways, she didn't think that she was too big for dolls.

'So I thought Magda might –'

She interrupted me. 'You'd let Magda play with her?'

'Well, I thought I'd let her . . . you know . . . keep her.'

Tears actually came to Mary's eyes. 'That's the kindest thing I've ever heard of,' she said, as she led the way, almost running, to Magda's cabin.

Magda was sitting on her bed when we opened the door to the cabin. I held the doll towards her. Magda's eyes opened wide, but otherwise she didn't move.

'Here,' I said. 'This is for you.'

Still she didn't move. Her mother shook her head as if in protest, but Mary smiled at her. 'It's all right,' she said.

Magda's mother nodded. I rocked the doll for a second then placed it gently in Magda's arms. Magda copied my action, rocking the doll carefully, like it was a real baby.

'Tell her its name,' said Mary.

I thought quickly. 'Tilly,' I said. 'Her name is Tilly.'

Then I pointed at the doll's chest and said slowly, 'Tilly.'

'Ti-lly,' said Magda. Then a huge smile spread across her face.

I would have smiled too, if I hadn't been so busy trying to hold back my tears.

 **17**

It's funny how time flies when you're on a ship that you know is speeding towards an iceberg that is very likely going to be the death of you.

I slept in Mary's cabin again, and soon it was Saturday morning.

After breakfast, Mary and I went to sit on our favourite place on deck. She unfastened her hair and let it fly in the wind. I stopped her when she started to pin it up again.

'Wait,' I said. 'Let me plait it for you. I always plait Tilly's for her.'

'Your doll?'

I shook my head. 'No, not my doll. I have a friend called Tilly too.'

Suddenly I remembered something. I pulled up the sleeve of my dress and held out my charm bracelet, turning the charms so that Mary could see the tiny photographs inside.

'That's Tilly and me,' I said, feeling sad as I gazed at Tilly's grinning face. I remembered how we'd laughed that day and tried for ages to take pictures that we both liked.

Mary gasped. 'Photographs! I've never had my photograph taken.'

I thought of all the photos of Tilly and me that I have on my computer.

I thought of the wall behind my bed, where I've stuck hundreds of photographs.

I thought of my world, which was so different to the one where Mary lived.

'Tilly is pretty,' said Mary, interrupting my thoughts.

I nodded, not trusting myself to speak.

Mary settled back against my knees and I started to plait her hair.

'Tell me all about her,' she said.

'She . . .' I stopped.

I missed Tilly so much, I didn't know that I could talk about her, but Mary was waiting.

'She what?'

I took a deep breath. 'She . . .' I stopped again. 'It's too hard,' I whispered.

Mary misunderstood. How could she possibly imagine why I found it so hard to describe Tilly?

'It can be hard to describe someone who is close to you,' she said. 'Just tell me what she likes and I'll know what kind of a person she is.'

'OK,' I said. 'Tilly likes all kinds of stuff. She likes swimming. She likes climbing. She likes ice cream. She's the best person for telling jokes that I've ever known. She likes TV. She –'

'What's TV?'

Oops. Still, what did it matter now?

But how do you explain TV? How would you think that you would ever find yourself in a place where you had to explain TV?

I finished plaiting Mary's hair, and she turned to face me, waiting.

'Well,' I began. 'TV is short for television. We

have it in Dublin, but I gather it hasn't arrived in County Cork yet?'

Mary shook her head. 'I've never heard of it. Tell me what it is.'

'It's like a box. Or it used to be like a box, but now it's mostly flat, like a picture.'

'And what kind of a picture is it?'

'It can be anything. Think of anything in the whole wide world, and it could be on TV.'

'Like a baby, or a doll or a hat or an apple?'

I smiled. 'Yes, it could be any one of those, or even all of them at the same time. But the important thing is that it moves.'

'The box moves?'

'No, the box stays in the same place, but the picture moves. It's like . . .' I had a sudden flash of inspiration. 'It's like the movies.'

'What are movies?'

I sighed.

Weren't movies invented yet? Or were they invented, but news hadn't got as far as the village where Mary used to live?

'OK, forget about movies. Just try to imagine a picture that moves, and it tells a story, or sometimes it's a group of people in a house and you can watch them doing stuff, like having their breakfast and washing their teeth.'

'Like looking in someone's window?'

I nodded. 'Kind of.'

'But isn't that rude?'

I nodded. 'I suppose it is rude, really. But it's very popular where I come from.'

Mary looked bored.

It was funny. Back home, I spend as much time as possible in front of the TV, but now I couldn't even explain it properly.

'Forget about TV,' said Mary. 'It doesn't sound so good. I don't think it would ever be popular in Cork. Tell me a story instead. Do you know any good stories?'

I grinned. 'I know heaps of great stories. Did I tell you the one about the boy wizard with the scar on his forehead?'

Mary shook her head. 'I've never heard that one.'

I took a deep breath and began. 'There was once a boy called Harry Potter . . .'

When I'd finished my tale, Mary sighed.

'That was a wonderful story. Did you make it up yourself?'

'Er, not exactly. It's very —'

Mary laughed as she finished my sentence. 'I know, I know — it's very popular where you come from.'

Then she jumped up. 'Let's go inside,' she said. 'There's someone I'd like you to meet. Her name is Aggie.'

Aggie was sitting on her own in the big dining hall. She looked about twenty years old and, like all the other Third-Class passengers, she was wearing neat but shabby clothes.

We sat beside her and Mary introduced us.

'How are you today, Aggie?' Mary asked.

Aggie didn't answer. Instead her grey eyes filled with tears. 'I think I'll go and lie down in my cabin for a while,' she said. And then she hurried off, pressing a lace-trimmed hanky to her overflowing eyes.

'What on earth was that about?' I asked.

Mary sighed. 'Aggie's grandmother didn't want her to go to America and they had a big fight before Aggie left. They parted on bad terms. Aggie said things that she's sorry for now.'

'That's sad,' I agreed.

'I suggested that Aggie should write a letter apologizing to her grandmother as soon as she gets to New York.'

'Sounds like a good plan to me.'

Mary nodded. 'But Aggie said her grandmother is very old and sick. And the post from America to Ireland takes ages. Aggie's afraid her grandmother won't live long enough to get the letter.'

Hello? Have you seen the name on this ship? There's a danger that no one around here is going to live very long.

'Wow, that's really, really sad,' I said.

'It breaks my heart that we can't do anything to help her,' said Mary.

I gave a small smile. 'I'm not too sure about that,' I said. 'Let me just think for a minute.'

18

A while later, Mary led the way to Aggie's cabin. A tear-stained Aggie opened the door, and waved us inside.

We went into the cabin and I sat on the bed next to Aggie's big brown suitcase. While Aggie was clearing a space for Mary to sit, I examined the suitcase. There were two large luggage labels on the side – one with an address in New York, and the other with an address in Cork. I peeled the second label from the suitcase and slipped it into my pocket. I didn't know where Aggie was going to end up, but the suitcase's only destination was the bottom of the sea, and it didn't need any address label to get there.

'Mary has told me the whole story,' I said.

'And Lauren's going to help you,' said Mary.
Aggie tried to smile. 'Thank you,' she said. 'But
there's nothing you can do. My grandmother is
going to die without knowing how sorry I am for
what I said to her. No one can change that.'

'Lauren can,' said Mary with great confidence.

'How?'

Mary hesitated. 'She hasn't told me exactly how.
I trust her though, and I think you should too.'

Now they both turned towards me expectantly.

'What would you like to say to your grandmother,
Aggie?' I asked.

Aggie wrung her hands together as if she were
washing them with invisible soap.

'I don't know,' she whispered.

'Er . . . you need to help me out here, Aggie,'
I said. 'Just think for a minute. Imagine if your
grandmother were right here in this cabin, right
now, what would you say to her?'

'Em . . . how did you get here?'

I tried to hide my smile.

'OK, so maybe that wasn't the best approach.

Forget that stuff. Tell me what you'd like to say to your granny . . . you know . . . about the way you parted?'

Aggie wrung her hands again.

'I'd . . . I'd say . . . I'm sorry, Granny . . . and I didn't mean to say all those bad things . . . and I love you and –'

'OK. That's probably enough. We'll be back later. Don't you worry about a thing.'

We closed the door on a speechless Aggie, and Mary followed me as I raced through the corridors.

'What are you going to do?' she asked.

'Be patient,' I said. 'And then you'll see.'

At last we got to the linen cupboard. I opened the door.

'Coming?' I asked.

Mary hesitated. 'I . . . I will if you want.'

The look of absolute terror on her face betrayed what she really felt.

'It's OK,' I said. 'I can do this on my own. You go and check on Magda or Aggie or Baba or someone.'

She gave a sudden smile. 'I could go and check on your parents, if you like.'

'No,' I said quickly.

Mary looked hurt.

'No, thanks,' I said more gently. 'It's nice of you to offer, but I know they want to rest. Now, I'd better go and I'll see you back in the dining hall in a little while.'

Then I closed the cupboard door and set off on my journey.

I was getting to know my way around by now, so even with a quick detour to feed Saturn, I was quickly at my destination.

I smoothed my hair and straightened my dress, and then knocked sharply on the door.

It was opened by a kind-looking man in a smart uniform.

'What can I do for you, young lady?' he asked.

'I need to send a telegram,' I said.

'Do you indeed?' he replied. He reached into a desk behind him and handed me a page. 'Fill in what you want to say, then give me back the form and the money and I'll send it at once.'

'Er . . . how much is it?'

'Twelve and six for the first ten words.'

Was that a lot or a little? – I had no idea. It didn't matter much, as I didn't have any money anyway.

'What if it's an emergency?'

Like the way you can call 999 for free on your mobile.

'It's still twelve and six.'

I smiled my best smile. 'I seem to have mislaid my purse. Can you send the telegram now and I'll come back and pay you later?'

He smiled kindly. 'I'm very sorry, miss. I'd like to help you out, but I can't. That's more than my job's worth. Pay me first then I send the telegram, that's the way it works.'

I'd been afraid of that.

I put my head down and wandered back along the decks. Soon I came across Ernestine, still playing with her pretty dolls. She looked up when she saw me coming.

'Where's your kitty?' she asked.

Suddenly I had a wonderful idea.

'Have you got any money?' I asked.

She smiled. 'I've got lots and lots. Daddy gave me some, and Mummy gave me some and Auntie Florence gave me some and –'

'OK. OK, I get the message. Will you give me some?'

'What do you want money for?'

'It's a secret.'

'If I give you money, what will you give me?'

I hesitated. What could I give her?

'Will you give me your kitty?'

I sighed. 'I can't give you my kitty, but if you give me money, I'll bring you my kitty and you can hold him and stroke him.'

Ernestine reached for her basket. 'How much do you need?'

I scrunched up my eyes, trying to remember what the man had said. 'Eighteen,' I said in the end.

'Eighteen doesn't make any sense.'

I thought again. 'I'm sure it's eighteen. The man said twelve and six.'

Ernestine laughed so loud that I thought people would come running.

'Shhh,' I said. 'What's so funny?'

'Twelve and six is twelve shillings and sixpence,' she said. 'And I've got much more than that.'

'So give me twelve and six, and we're done here.'

Ernestine took ages counting out the money, but at last it was safe in my fist.

'I'll wait here for you and the kitty. Don't forget. You promised.'

'Sure,' I said. 'I'll bring the kitty here – if I get time.'

Then I skipped off before she could say anything more.

Filling in the telegram form took me ages. How do you convey what might be your last message ever to someone you love, in just ten words?

All the things I wanted to say – like *LOL* or *ILY* were totally useless, as there was zero chance of Aggie's granny understanding them.

In the end, I was fairly pleased with what I had done.

Sorry, Granny. Did not mean bad words. Love you. Aggie.

I handed the form and the money to the man.

'Address it to "Aggie's granny",' I said. 'She lives at . . .'

'Aggie's granny?' the man repeated. 'That's a funny name.'

'I know,' I said, feeling a bit stupid.

Then he wrote 'Aggie's granny' on a slip of paper, and followed it with the address I read aloud from the label I'd torn off Aggie's suitcase.

A few minutes later the man handed me back the page. SENT APRIL 13TH 1912 was stamped over my words.

'Thank you, so, so much,' I said.

The man looked embarrassed. 'All in a day's work,' he said as he turned back to his desk.

Aggie cried when I handed her the receipt and told her what I'd done. 'You've made me the happiest woman on the ship,' she said. 'My granny's never got a telegram before. She'll be the talk of the parish.'

Then she tried to kiss my hands, but that was way too weird, so I made my excuses, and Mary and I left.

As soon as we were safely in the corridor, Mary turned to me.

'I don't know how you managed that, but you are very brave.'

I shook my head. 'Brave is easy. I could never be as kind as you.'

Now she shook her head. 'You *are* kind. And you're brave and honest and . . .'

Now I felt really bad. Had she any idea how many lies I had told her?

My parents are asleep in a cabin just along the corridor?

When I pretend to visit my parents, I'm really visiting a weird time-travelling cat, who's been hiding in a lifeboat for the last few days?

I made up the best bits of Harry Potter?

Mary took my hands in hers. 'I can tell these things,' she said. 'And I can tell that you've got an honest soul.'

Now I felt really, really bad.

But then I remembered that there was one honest thing I could do.

*

A few minutes later, I was edging along the quietest deck I'd been able to find.

'Ready?' I asked.

'Ready,' said Ernestine, holding out her hands.

I unwrapped the big bath towel and Ernestine gasped.

'Kitty!'

Saturn patiently endured Ernestine's tight hugs and sloppy kisses. We were only rescued when the shrill voice of Ernestine's mother came to us on the wind.

'Ernestine. Where *have* you got to?'

Ernestine gave Saturn one last kiss and handed him back to me.

'I have to go,' she said sadly. 'It's time for my bath.'

I wished it was time for my bath.

I smiled at her. 'Know what, Ernestine? You're not so bad, really.'

She smiled happily back at me and skipped off towards her mother.

19

I ate my evening meal with Mary and her family. I felt sad as I played with Baba, and made up answers to Mary's mother's concerned questions about my parents.

I wondered why no one else seemed to be bothered by the smell. In the warm air, the whiff of greasy hair and sweaty bodies was pretty bad. (Still, since I hadn't washed properly in days, I probably didn't smell that sweet either.)

After we'd finished eating, Mary and I went for a walk.

'Only four more days till I see my daddy,' she said.

I'd been listening to this talk for two days now, but still it made me feel sick and sad.

Suddenly I had a wonderful idea.

'There's something I've got to do,' I said. 'I'll meet you back in the cabin in a bit, OK?'

Mary was used to my sudden disappearances so she didn't argue.

As I ran, I felt both happy and stupid. Why hadn't I thought of it before?

The kind radio operator was surprised to see me again.

'Another telegram?' he joked. 'Is it for Aggie's grandfather this time?'

I shook my head. 'Be serious,' I said. 'I have something very important to tell you.'

He put on a serious face, but I was fairly sure that he was just humouring me.

I took a minute to plan my words. My last two approaches hadn't worked so I knew I had to try something different. I remembered my dad telling me once that when the *Titanic* sank, there was another ship nearby that could have saved everyone. Only trouble was, the other ship's radio officer was asleep, and when he woke up and learned about the tragedy, it was already much too late.

'Are you on duty tomorrow night?' I asked.

Now the man looked really surprised. 'I am, actually. Are you asking me for a date? I think I'm a bit old for you, don't you?'

'No,' I said fiercely. 'I'm not asking you for a date. It's just that . . .' I hesitated, trying to find the right words.

'Go on,' he said gently.

'Tomorrow night,' I said in the end. 'There are going to be icebergs in the sea, aren't there?'

He nodded. 'There usually are at this time of year, but that's not a problem to a ship like this.'

'But *if* we hit an iceberg, we could all be saved if there was a ship nearby, couldn't we?'

'This is one of the busiest shipping lanes in the world. There are always other ships nearby.'

'But are the radio people on those ships on duty all night?'

'No,' he conceded.

'So when, I mean, *if* you need help they will all be asleep.'

'But . . .'

'So tomorrow night, the dangerous night, you have to persuade all the other radio people on all the other ships to stay awake. You have to think of a way. You could call it a radio party. You could take turns telling jokes, or you could have a quiz or something.'

I felt sure I was sounding pathetic, and something in the man's eyes made me feel that he thought the same. I couldn't give up, though.

'Just make sure that they are all listening,' I said. 'So if we hit an iceberg, you could let the other ships know at once and they could come and rescue us.'

He smiled. 'Sounds like you read too many adventure stories,' he said. 'But you're forgetting one thing. The *Titanic* is unsinkable. Even if we did hit an iceberg, it wouldn't matter. Now, it's been nice talking to you, but I have work to do. I have telegrams to send.'

I wished I had enough money to send a telegram to myself. I could send it care of my great-granny. It could be passed down through the family like an heirloom, until it got to me. This is what I'd write:

```
DEAR LAUREN. WHEN YOU ARE TWELVE, IF YOU
MEET A STRANGE OLD LADY IN A PARK AND SHE
TRIES TO GIVE YOU HER CAT — DON'T TAKE
IT.
```

'Please,' I said to the man. 'Please listen to me.'

He turned to go.

I was all out of ideas and I knew this was my last chance.

In desperation, I got down on my knees and begged. 'You *have* to listen to me,' I said. 'Hundreds of lives are at stake.'

Now the man looked really embarrassed. 'Get up,' he said. 'You're –'

He stopped talking and I followed his gaze along the corridor. The captain was walking towards us with three big, strong-looking sailors beside him.

'You again,' said the captain, beginning to walk faster. 'You're becoming a bit of a menace.'

I scrambled to my feet. No one was ever going to believe me. Now I knew that for sure.

I spoke to the radio officer. 'I remember you from the movie.'

'Movie?'

'Yes. And you'll be glad to know they got a really cool guy to play your part.'

'Play my part?'

'Well, whatever. Tomorrow night, do what you can, but don't forget to save yourself. You're a nice man and none of this is your fault.'

He started to say something, but I had no time to hang around to hear it – the captain and his heavy-men were almost beside us.

So I picked up the skirts of Mikey's mother's dress and ran for my life.

 **20**

That night I climbed into the top bunk in
Mary's cabin again. Her mother and Baba
were already asleep.

'Tell me another story,' said Mary.

I told her all about Tracy Beaker and she clapped
her hands softly when I was finished.

'You make up the best stories ever,' she said.
Then she turned over to go to sleep.

I lay in the darkness, listening to the loud
throbbing of the ship's engines and all at once, I
knew I couldn't stay there. This wasn't my story.
I had to escape and go to Saturn. I had to find a
way to make him take me home again. And I
wasn't leaving him until he did so. And if that

failed, at least I'd be in a lifeboat when the trouble started.

But there was one thing I had to do first.

Mary and I stood together in the corridor outside her cabin. She rubbed her eyes.

'I was asleep, Lauren,' she said. 'Why did you wake me up? And why did we have to come out here?'

'This is important,' I said. 'And I didn't want your mother to hear. But please say goodbye to her and Baba for me.'

'Goodbye?' she repeated, sounding puzzled. 'Sure won't you be seeing them in the morning?'

I avoided her question.

Was it selfish of me to hope that I'd never see them again?

'I have to go somewhere,' I said. 'And if I don't come back . . .'

Suddenly I hugged Mary. She seemed embarrassed, but she didn't pull away.

I could feel her shoulder-bones through the thin fabric of her nightdress. She felt frail and thin.

How could I abandon her? How could I find a way to help her?

At last I let her go and stared into her eyes.

'You and me – we're friends, right?' I said.

She nodded uncertainly. 'Yes, and we're still going to be friends when we get to New York. Remember you promised?'

I hadn't promised, actually, but I ignored this. I was trying to find a way to show Mary how serious I was.

I put my hands to my face in an effort to concentrate. As I did so, one of my charms snagged in my hair. Mary helped me to untangle it, and I suddenly had an idea. I loosened the narrow silver link and took the charm off the bracelet. It was a tiny heart, with FRIENDS engraved on one side. I twirled it around and saw the single word on the other side – FOREVER.

'Tilly gave me this,' I said.

'Then it must be very special to you,' said Mary.

'It is,' I said, remembering how happy I'd been the day Tilly had given it to me. She'd been almost shy as she handed it over.

'I know it's not your birthday or anything,' she'd said. 'But I saw this and thought of you . . . so . . . here . . . this is for you.'

And when I'd opened the tiny box, I'd had to wipe away a totally embarrassing tear and pretend that I had dust in my eye, and I'd hugged Tilly, and she'd hugged me back, and everything had been perfect.

I totally loved this charm, but that wasn't important now. This could be a matter of life and death.

I held the charm towards Mary.

'I'd like you to have it,' I said.

Mary looked puzzled. 'I couldn't take it from you. It wouldn't be right.'

I held it towards her. 'I want you to have it.'

Still she resisted. 'What would Tilly say if she knew you gave it away?'

I wondered that too.

'I think she'd understand,' I said.

If I ever see her again to explain.

Mary shook her head. 'It's beautiful, but I can't take it from you.'

'You can and you must,' I said so fiercely that she took a step backwards.

'Tilly gave me this charm,' I said. 'And now I'm giving it to you. It's like a chain of friendship through the ages.'

'Ages? How long have you had this?' asked Mary.

'Oh, a while,' I said vaguely. 'But that doesn't matter now. What matters is that you must keep this charm with you at all times. It's to remind you.'

'To remind me of you? I don't need a charm for that. Even when I get to New York, I won't ever forget you.'

This was getting too sad and too complicated, but I couldn't stop now. 'I won't ever forget you, either, Mary, but that's not the point. If something bad happens to this ship, you must look at the charm and it will be like a trigger, to make you remember.'

'Make me remember you? I already said –'

I shook my head. 'No, it's not to make you remember me; well, not just for that. I'm giving you the charm so that when . . . if something goes

171

wrong on this ship, you'll remember what I'm going to tell you next.'

She shook her head. 'This is the *Titanic*. Nothing's going to go wrong. Nothing bad is going to happen.'

'Please, Mary,' I whispered, trying not to cry.

This was all too hard. Why had I ended up on the *Titanic*?

Why couldn't I have ended up on a pleasure cruiser on the river Shannon, or on the ferry in Waterford, where my family went on holidays one time?

But wishing wasn't going to help me, and it wasn't going to do Mary a whole lot of good, either.

'Take the charm,' I said as firmly as I could manage. 'And listen to me.'

'If that's what you want,' said Mary, sounding a bit scared. Her hand shook a little as she reached out and took the charm from me. She slowly closed her fingers over it.

'Thank you,' she whispered.

'You're welcome,' I said. 'And now you have to listen very carefully. Don't argue any more. Just listen.'

172

She nodded gravely.

I tried not to care that Mary probably thought her new best friend had just gone crazy, as I spoke as clearly and as carefully as I could.

'Tomorrow night this ship is going to hit an iceberg, and a few hours after that, it's going to sink.'

'But –'

I shook my head to silence her. 'When . . . if that happens, look at this charm, and think of me. Then remember what I am telling you now. And then you must act very quickly. You must find your mother and Baba and take them to that storeroom I showed you. Do you remember where it is?'

She nodded.

'And you must go through the door that leads to the First-Class area.'

'But we're not allowed up there. What if someone sees us? I'd be too afraid.'

I shook my head again. 'Don't worry about that – you will have worse things to be afraid of if you don't go up there, I promise you. Just listen, Mary, and do what I say. Don't wait for anyone to help you because they probably won't. And you must act the minute you feel a bump or hear a siren, or any other signal that something might be going wrong. Then the three of you – you and your mother and Baba – must go to one of the First-Class decks and make sure that you get into a lifeboat. They will let you in because of Baba, and then you'll be safe. Everyone who gets into a lifeboat will be safe.'

'But –'

Then I remembered something else from the film. 'And don't worry about taking someone else's place in a lifeboat. Lots of the boats will be launched when they're only half full. So if you don't jump in, no one else will either – and imagine what a waste that would be.'

Mary's face had turned even paler than usual.

'You're frightening me, Lauren,' she said.

I tried to smile, but failed. This *sooo* wasn't a time for smiles.

'I'm sorry, Mary,' I said. 'I'm sorry I have to frighten you, and I'm sorry that I've made you think that I'm crazy.'

Mary didn't deny thinking I was crazy, and that made me sad, but I continued to speak.

'But please, Mary, promise me that you'll do what I say.'

'You're telling me to save Mammy and Baba and myself? What about Magda and her parents, and Aggie, and . . .'

I should have known that Mary wouldn't forget all of her new friends.

'Whatever,' I said. 'Bring whoever you like, but promise me that you'll go yourself.'

Suddenly she looked stubborn. 'I don't believe you,' she said. 'The ship isn't going to sink and I won't have to save anyone. I don't know why you're acting like this, since we're supposed to be friends, but I think you're just trying to scare me. Nothing bad is going to happen.'

I sighed. This was turning out to be harder than I had feared. '*If* something happens, will you do as I say, Mary? Please?'

She nodded slowly. 'Only because we're best friends.'

I tried to smile. 'Yes,' I whispered. 'We're best friends.'

As I turned away, she caught my arm.

'Wait,' she said. 'You gave me a present, so I have to give you one.'

She unfastened a blue ribbon from round her neck. On it hung a small silver-coloured disc.

She held it towards me. 'Here,' she said. 'You can have my holy medal.'

I shook my head. 'No way. I'm not taking your holy medal.'

If you're ever going to need a holy medal, it's going to be tomorrow night.

'It's all right,' she said. 'My mother has lots more. All of our friends gave them to us, to bring us happiness in our new lives in America.'

Then she put her hands round my neck and tied the ribbon.

I hugged her again. 'Friends forever,' I said.

'Friends forever,' she repeated, and then I pulled away and ran as fast I could towards the linen cupboard.

 **21**

I opened the cupboard door and slipped inside.
'Passengers aren't allowed in here.'

It was a girl who didn't look much older than me. There was another girl beside her and they were busy folding sheets. Both girls were dressed in blue uniforms.

'Sorry,' I muttered, as I backed out the way I had come.

I stood in the corridor for ages, waiting for them to finish. I could hear the girls laughing as they worked, telling each other stories about their boyfriends.

I was gripped with a sudden sense of panic.

What if Saturn was gone? What if he'd gone back to the future without me?

And still the girls chattered on. 'Jimmy's such a rogue,' said one. 'I said to him, "What kind of a fool do you take me for?" And he said, "A very pretty fool." And I said, "How dare you?" And then he kissed me.'

They both laughed.

Very funny, but I can't hang around here forever, I've got to try and persuade my cat to take me time-travelling.

At last the cupboard door opened again. I peeped round a corner and watched the girls strolling down the corridor. Then I raced through the cupboard and up on to the First-Class decks.

It was dark and cold outside. I breathed deeply, wondering if it was possible to smell ice. I felt scared and alone. This whole thing was much, much too scary for a twelve-year-old.

Saturn was sitting exactly where I had left him, inside lifeboat number seven. I climbed up, pulled the heavy covering aside and sat next to him. The blue and green stones on his collar sparkled in the light from the deck.

He sniffed my fingers.

'No, Saturn,' I said firmly. 'I didn't bring any food. Food would be a distraction. I need you to concentrate on taking me back to where I belong in time.'

There was no way my life's plan had ever included any of this. For some reason, I would never have imagined myself sitting on the *Titanic*, talking to a strange, hairy, white cat, trying to persuade it to take me home.

But nothing of what had happened lately had been part of my life's plan, and if begging a cat to help me was all I could think of doing – well, that's what I was going to do.

Unfortunately Saturn didn't seem interested. He just kept sniffing my pockets in a vain search for food.

'No food,' I said sharply.

Saturn gazed at me with his superior look.

'Remember me? I'm Lauren. I'm the girl who took you in when Betsy abandoned you. You owe me. You –' I began, before stopping suddenly. I could hear footsteps and two male voices. The footsteps stopped right underneath the lifeboat.

179

'Did you hear a noise from that lifeboat?' asked one of the voices.

'I think perhaps I did,' replied the other.

I held my breath and glared at Saturn. This *soooo* wasn't the time for one of his loud miaows.

Then one of the men gave a deep chuckle. 'It's probably just two young sweethearts. We should leave them in peace.'

The other man sighed. 'Oh, to be young again.'

Both men laughed and then the footsteps began again, before fading slowly into the distance.

I glared at Saturn. Two young sweethearts – ha! I felt like strangling him for getting me into this mess.

Then I felt sorry for that thought. I loved Saturn more than I had loved any pet ever. And whatever this whole time-travel thing was about, it was hardly his fault.

And surely, if Saturn had a choice in the matter, he'd prefer to be lying in the sunshine in our back garden, looking forward to a big meal of his favourite special food.

So I picked Saturn up and cuddled him for a long time as I tried to figure out what to do next.

An icy breeze was blowing. I thought longingly of my warm fleece. I hoped it was already wrapped in tissue paper in Mikey's attic, waiting for his first little girl to come along.

Saturn seemed to be dozing off, so I shook him gently.

'Wake up!' I said. 'Don't you understand? We're in the wrong time. We don't belong here, you and me. We belong in the future. You know – the place with computers and TVs and fancy dried cat food.'

Saturn seemed unimpressed, but I had to keep trying.

'Please, Saturn,' I said. 'This ship is called the *Titanic*. You were curled up in Tilly's arms the last time we watched the DVD. Weren't you paying any attention at all? This ship is going to sink! Remember how all the people clung on until the last minute? Remember the huge scary drop down to the water? I'm afraid of heights and you hate water. It's going to be both of our worst nightmares come true.'

181

Saturn blinked once.

'I don't really understand what's going on,' I said.
'I've no idea how I got here, but I know it's got
something to do with you. You made strange things
happen when you were living with Betsy, and you
probably did the same to the poor man who owned
you before Betsy came along. So now, you're the one
who has to get us out of here. There isn't a Plan B.
This is it. You're my only hope.'

Saturn just stared at me with his shiny green and
blue eyes.

I started to cry. 'I miss Mum and Dad, and Tilly,'
I wailed. 'I even miss Amy and Stephen. I miss my
life. I'm afraid and I want to go home.'

Tears poured down my face and dripped on to
Saturn's fur. He licked them off, seeming surprised
at their salty taste.

'You'd better get used to it,' I said bitterly. 'Soon
you'll have lots and lots of salty water on your fur,
and it'll be too late then.'

Saturn blinked.

'And it'll be worse for you,' I said. 'I might be able

to stay in this lifeboat. It's women and children first, but I bet there won't be any room for cats – even beautiful designer ones like you.'

Saturn gave a soft *miaow*. Then he snuggled deeper into my arms, closed his eyes and fell asleep.

'Thanks for nothing, pal,' I muttered.

I sat there, blinking in the icy wind. One of the stones from Saturn's collar was pressing into my arm. I moved to make myself more comfortable and Saturn whimpered in his sleep. And then . . .

22

'Lauren, stop being so lazy! Come in here and help me to tidy up the kitchen.'

Mum?

I was sitting on the living-room floor, with Saturn in my arms. But how could that be?

I looked down and saw that Mikey's mother's dress was gone and I was wearing my old T-shirt and shorts.

Upstairs I could hear Amy's music still pounding away; from the study, I could hear Stephen shouting at the computer.

Mum was standing in the doorway. 'Don't make me ask you a second time,' she said.

'Mum!' I cried.

I put Saturn on the carpet, jumped up and ran over to her. I threw my arms round her neck. Then I clung on like I never wanted to let go.

Mum laughed. 'It's always nice to get hugs, but don't you think this is a bit over the top?'

I just squeezed her tighter. She was so solid and real and comforting that I never wanted to let her go.

'Mum, I'm so sorry,' I said. 'I know you must have been worried, but it wasn't my fault – honestly. It just happened. I think it was Saturn's fault, but I don't really understand how. And I've been so scared . . . and I've missed you and Dad so much . . . and I didn't know how I was going to get out of there . . . and I was so afraid . . . and my phone wouldn't work . . . and I know it's been days and days . . . and . . . I don't even care if you punish me . . . You can do whatever you like and I won't mind . . . I'm just glad to be back.'

Mum used both of her hands to untangle my arms from round her neck. She stared into my eyes and I was so happy to see her worried face that I thought I was going to cry.

'Lauren, have you bumped your head or something?'

'No. I was just sitting here brushing Saturn, when –'

'It's OK, darling,' she whispered. 'You must have dozed off for a minute and had a bad dream.'

I know that in books and movies stuff like this always turns out to have been a dream. Once Tilly ended an essay by saying 'and then I woke up' and our teacher got really cross.

'That's a cop-out, Tilly,' the teacher said. 'You'd better think of a different ending, or else you'll have to write a whole new story.'

But that *sooo* wasn't what had happened to me.

'No, Mum,' I said. 'It wasn't a dream. It really happened. I know it did. I met Mikey and then I met Mary, and they were real. They were as real as you are. I could talk to them and touch them, and we did loads of stuff together, for days and days and days. And then we were on the *Titanic* –'

Mum raised one eyebrow. 'The *Titanic*?'

'Yes. I know it sounds crazy, but it wasn't a dream.'

Mum stroked my forehead. 'I know, darling,' she said. 'It wasn't a dream. It sounds more like a nightmare, but it's over now. You're safe here with me.'

'No,' I protested again. 'It really happened. Saturn was with me.'

Mum turned round and pointed to Saturn, who was sleeping peacefully.

'I know it wasn't a dream,' I repeated.

'I understand, Lauren,' she said, smiling. She didn't even bother trying to sound convincing. 'But you have to remember, when you're young, dreams can sometimes be very vivid. I think it's something to do with hormones.'

Usually when Mum mentions hormones, it ends up in a totally embarrassing conversation, but I wasn't worried about that now. I just had to make her understand what had happened to me.

'But I was gone for days and days,' I said.

I tried to count back, but I was too confused to do it properly. The past and the present kept getting mixed up.

'It was two or three days or something like that,' I said in the end.

Mum looked at her watch. 'You remember the chocolate cake I was making?'

I nodded. It seemed like it had happened a very long time ago, but I could remember scraping the chocolatey mix from the side of the bowl – and Mum taking the bowl from me before I was finished with it.

'Well,' said Mum. 'The cake went into the oven at quarter past three, and it's half past now. It's only been fifteen minutes since I saw you. That's not a lot of time for adventures, is it?'

'But . . .'

Mum sighed. 'Is this all an excuse so you don't have to help me tidy the kitchen?'

Tears came to my eyes at the injustice of it all.

Mum hugged me again. 'Dear me, Lauren,' she said. 'You are having a bad day. How about I ask Amy to help me in the kitchen?'

I nodded slowly, not trusting myself to say any more.

Mum smiled. 'Now I have to go and check on the cake. You lie on the couch for a while, and when the cake is done, I'll bring you in a big slice while it's still lovely and warm. How does that sound?'

It sounded a whole lot better than sitting on a cold, dark ship, waiting for the sickening sound of ice against steel.

'Thanks, Mum,' I said.

I was still in the living room when Tilly called over later.

She threw herself on to the floor next to Saturn and began to stroke his head.

'How come you're not answering your phone?' she asked.

I put my hand into my pocket and pulled out my phone.

'The battery's dead,' I said, blinking away the sudden image of me lying on the top bunk in Mary's cabin, watching as the last bar of battery faded away.

I went to the dresser, pulled out my charger and plugged in my phone. It flashed on immediately.

Sending failed.

Retry?

Then I saw the message I'd tried to send Mum.

Sorry, Mum. On the Titanic. Home ASAP.

I deleted the message and sat down, feeling suddenly weak. Tilly was staring at me.

'Your mum says you're not feeling very well,' she said. 'And she's right. Your face is whiter than Saturn's fur.'

'You're never going to believe what happened to me this afternoon,' I said.

'What?' she said.

'I was sitting here, combing Saturn, and then –'

Suddenly it all seemed too crazy.

I'm not a freak. I'm a normal kid. What was I doing thinking I had travelled back in time? Even trying to put it into words seemed impossible. Mum was right after all – the whole thing must have been an unusually vivid dream – so vivid that I'd tried to text back to reality in the middle of it.

'Forget it,' I said to Tilly, who had probably forgotten it already. 'How did you get on in your cousin's house?'

A while later, Tilly stood up. 'I need to go home for dinner,' she said.

I stood up too and followed her into the hall.

'Hey,' she said, as I raised my hand to open the front door. 'Where's the charm I gave you?'

I could see she wasn't happy and I couldn't blame her.

'I thought you were going to keep that charm forever – even when you are married,' she said. 'So much for your promises.'

I looked at the gap on my bracelet. Then we went back and we both looked on the couch where I'd been sitting, but there was no sign of the charm.

I closed my eyes for a second and saw Mary's thin fingers closing over it.

'I'm sorry, Tilly. I . . .' I began, not knowing how to finish.

Tilly stepped closer.

'And what's that weird thing round your neck?' she asked.

I moved my hand slowly towards my neck, but before it got there, I knew exactly what it was going to find – a small, silver-coloured disc hanging from a narrow blue ribbon.

 **23**

I slept a lot over the next few days. But no matter how much I slept, I still felt more tired than I had ever felt before.

One afternoon, I took Mary's medal from its blue ribbon and clipped it into the new space on my charm bracelet. It wasn't as bright and shiny as my other charms, but looking at it comforted me in a way that nothing else did.

Many times I thought of telling Mum or Dad or Tilly about what had happened to me, but I couldn't do it.

It was all too weird – and I don't do weird.

Stephen might have believed me, but he believes all kinds of crazy stuff, so that wouldn't have counted.

Sometimes I looked at Saturn, like he'd be able to help me.

Did he remember what had happened? Did he have any idea how much weird stuff had gone on recently?

One morning I even mashed up some bread and milk and put it into Saturn's bowl to see if it would jog his memory about being in Ballyboher. He sniffed the food for a while and then gazed at me for so long that I almost managed to convince myself that he was grinning at me.

'Get real,' I imagined him saying. 'We're not in 1912 any more, you know.'

And then he curled up and went to sleep – it looked like time-travelling was tiring for him too.

Sometimes Tilly and I went to the park, and I sat on a bench while she did her extreme climbing thing. I half hoped that Betsy would show up. There were lots of things I needed to ask her.

Did she end up on the *Titanic* too? Or did she go to a totally different time and place? Was this time-travelling stuff finished now, or could it happen again any minute? Should I go around all the time with my pockets stuffed with emergency time-travelling supplies?

And I wanted to tell Betsy that she hadn't been crazy at all. That she hadn't imagined things. That Saturn really was a very strange cat.

But Betsy never showed up again.

I couldn't forget my time with Mikey and Mary. Often, something funny would happen and I'd think, I must tell Mary that. But then I realized that I was never going to see Mary, or tell her anything, ever again.

It was like I'd been watching a film that had stopped just before the end. Or like I'd been reading a book and discovered that the last few pages were missing.

I had to know how the story finished.

Except that this was even worse. Mikey and Mary weren't just dull names from a history book, or characters invented for a film. They were real people.

I knew what their voices were like. I knew what made them laugh and what made them sad. I knew what they were afraid of, and what they dreamed of. I knew everything about them – except what happened next.

I spent a lot of time on the Internet. I got very excited when I found the 1901 and 1911 censuses. I quickly found the pages for Ballyboher, and seconds later I found the Spillane family. I felt a sudden pang in my chest when I saw the names written on the screen.

In 1901 there were four names:

Bridget Spillane – Female Aged 64 years
James Spillane – Male Aged 27 years
Nora Spillane – Female Aged 25 years
Michael Spillane – Male infant

By 1911 there were only two names left:

Bridget Spillane – Female Aged 74 years
Michael Spillane – Male Aged 10 years

Mikey's mother must have been dead by then, and his father must already have been in Scotland. The small, lonely family was reduced to two lines of print in scrawly handwriting.

And what happened after that?

Did Mikey get home safely from the *Titanic*? Did he sow the carrots and the potatoes and live happily ever after?

Or . . .?

The Internet had loads of sites with information on the *Titanic*. Funnily enough, none of them mentioned a strange girl from the future, or her even stranger, odd-eyed cat.

I soon learned that the reason I'd never heard of Queenstown before was that some time after the *Titanic* it was renamed Cobh.

It didn't surprise me to learn that Ernestine and her mother survived and went on to become hugely rich in America. And it didn't take me long to discover that there were lots of people called Mary on the *Titanic*. Some of them survived and some of

197

them didn't, but I didn't know enough about my friend Mary to figure out if she was one of the lucky ones. I never knew her surname, or her mother's name, and for all I knew her little baby brother didn't even live long enough to have a name of his own.

Mary and her family wouldn't have had much of a chance – unless she'd remembered what I had told her.

I became obsessed with finding out what had happened to Mary. I had to know if I'd been able to help her. I had to know if she'd made it to New York and if she'd fulfilled her vision of becoming a hat designer . . . or if all her dreams had come to a watery end not long after we last met.

Sometimes, I wasn't sure why it mattered so much to me. After all, Mary had to be dead by now, so why should I care if she died ninety years ago, or just last week?

But somehow, it did matter. It mattered more than anything else in my life.

*

Then one morning Mum came into my bedroom. She sat on the edge of my bed and stroked my hair.

'I'm worried about you, Lauren,' she said. 'You haven't been yourself for the past few days. Is there anything you'd like to tell me?'

I shook my head. I'd made up my mind that the whole time-travel thing was far too weird and complicated to share with anyone else.

'I'm fine,' I lied.

I knew Mum didn't believe me.

'Maybe we should get away for a while,' she said.

I didn't answer. I'd been away for quite long enough already, thank you very much.

'Maybe a change would be good for you,' she said. 'Maybe a few days by the sea would bring the colour back to your cheeks. Tilly can come with us, if you like. Stephen's scout camp starts tomorrow and Amy's going to stay at Tara's, so it would just be the three of us.'

'No,' I said. 'I don't want to go anywhere.'

She ignored me. 'Susan has rented a cottage by the sea. She's invited us to visit for a few days.'

I groaned. Mum's sister Susan is OK, but her geeky son Adrian is a total pain.

'No,' I said more forcefully.

Once again Mum ignored me.

'It's in Cork. And Susan –'

'What did you say?'

'It's in Cork. Susan has rented a house just outside Cork city.'

'Is that near Quee– I mean Cobh?'

'Well, sort of. It's not a million miles away.'

'Well, maybe yes,' I said. 'I'll go if we can visit Cobh while we're there.'

Mum wrinkled her eyebrows. 'Why do you suddenly want to visit Cobh?'

'I . . . I . . . I just do.'

Mum sighed. 'Sounds a bit strange to me, but since this is the first thing you've shown any interest in for a whole week, I'm not going to argue with you.'

I hugged her. 'Thanks, Mum,' I said.

'You're welcome,' she replied. 'Now get up and give Tilly a call to see if she can come with us.'

24

'I wish we could have brought Saturn,' I sighed.
    'He'd have hated the car journey,' said Mum.
'Don't you remember the fuss he made when we
took him to the vet's for his check-up?'

'I know, but –'

'But what?' asked Tilly.

*But Saturn and I have been through so much together, and
now it feels strange not being near him.*

'But nothing,' I said.

'Don't worry, Lauren,' said Mum. 'Dad's dying to
have Saturn to himself for a few days. That cat will
be totally spoiled by the time we get home.'

Tilly laughed. 'He's totally spoiled already.
Anyway, Deirdre, are we nearly there?'

'Only a few more miles to go,' said Mum. 'We can have lunch when we get there. You girls must be starving.'

'I'm absolutely ravenous,' said Tilly.

'Me too,' I said. 'I could eat a . . . OMIGOD! Stop the car!'

The car screeched to a halt and I jumped out, quickly followed by Mum and Tilly. I stood by the side of the road, trembling. Tilly rubbed my back and Mum pulled a bundle of tissues from the glove compartment.

'It's OK, darling,' said Mum. 'Do you feel sick?'

I shook my head. 'No, I'm fine.'

'You don't look fine,' said Tilly. 'You look like you've just seen a ghost.'

That *sooo* wasn't funny.

I pointed to the signpost that had caused this crisis.

'Can we go there?' I said to Mum.

Mum sighed. 'I thought you wanted to go to Cobh.'

'I do,' I said. 'I totally do. But first can we go to Ballyboher?'

I tried to interpret the look that passed between

Mum and Tilly. I think it was a *We've-tried-to-be-understanding-about-your-weird-behaviour-lately-but-there-is-a-limit-and-it-looks-like-maybe-we've-reached-that-limit* look.

Mum smiled a worried smile. 'Why on earth do you want to go there?' she asked. She already thought I was crazy, so there was no way I was telling anything close to the truth. I thought quickly.

'Er . . . in history last year . . . there was a whole chapter about this guy . . . I forget his name, though . . . and he was from Ballyboher . . . and because I did a special project on him, our teacher said if I was ever anywhere nearby I should go and visit his birthplace.'

'What guy?' asked Tilly.

'You know . . . the . . . the famous guy,' I said pathetically.

Tilly rolled her eyes. She's much better at history than I am and we both knew that if we had studied a famous guy from Ballyboher, she would have remembered it perfectly well. But she's a good friend, so she smiled as if she had the faintest idea of what I was talking about.

'Oh, that guy,' she said. 'I remember him now.'

'What was he famous for?' asked Mum with narrow, suspicious eyes.

Tilly smiled sweetly. 'He was a hero in the Bolivian revolution of 1872.'

I put my head down to hide my smile. I was fairly sure that Tilly had just invented the Bolivian revolution of 1872.

Mum sighed as we all climbed back into the car.

'I suppose it's not too far. But ten minutes only, Lauren, and then we're going on to Cobh, OK?'

I nodded. Mum started the car, reversed a little and took the turn for Ballyboher.

Seconds later, I screeched again. 'Stop the car!'

Mum stopped the car, but this time I was the only one who got out. I knew I was pushing things with Mum and Tilly, but I couldn't help it.

I walked across the small road, hardly daring to breathe.

The roof and the windows and the doors were gone, but there was no mistaking it – this was Mikey's house. I looked back at the car. Mum and

Tilly were sitting with folded arms and *not-very-patient* looks on their faces.

I smiled an apologetic smile and stepped inside the building. I put my hands over my face and tried not to cry.

I could almost smell the turf fire that had warmed me up on that strange day – my first day in 1912.

Above the birdsong, I imagined that I could almost hear Mikey's laughter in my ears. I half expected to see Granny Bridget sitting on her old rocking chair, knitting, and Mikey sitting by the window. I half expected to see Saturn eating his bowl of bread and milk.

But all I could see were cobwebs, and weeds and decay.

What had happened to the big kitchen table and the trunk, containing Mikey's mother's precious clothes? What had happened to Mikey?

I walked back outside, wishing there was a door that I could close behind me.

When I got back to the car, Mum and Tilly had

forced, *We're-being-very-patient* looks on their faces. I knew that they had been talking about me.

I wished I could tell them everything.

I wished there was a way of making them understand.

But I knew there was no point.

I could still almost taste Granny Bridget's greasy bacon in my mouth.

I could still almost hear Mikey's happy laughter ringing in my ears.

But, even so, *I* could hardly believe my own story. So how could I possibly hope to convince them?

25

Mum started the car.

'There's just one more small thing before we go to Cobh,' I said.

'What?' asked Mum, trying to sound patient even though I knew she didn't feel that way.

'Can we drive into the village, please?'

Mum didn't answer, but she put the car into gear and we drove slowly towards the village of Ballyboher. We stopped on the only street and I climbed out of the car.

'Won't be long,' I said.

No one answered.

*

Last time round I'd never made it this far, and now I couldn't bring myself to feel disappointed about that. It was like the village that time forgot. There was one shop with a few faded packets of cereal in the window, about six houses and a church.

The shop was closed and the houses looked empty, so I walked towards the church. I pushed open a small gate, wincing as it squeaked loudly. The church door was closed, so I walked round to the back of the building. I realized that I was approaching a small graveyard. If there were answers to my questions, I knew they had to be here.

I walked slowly along the grassy paths. Some of the gravestones were toppling sideways, like the effort of standing up straight was too much for them. Some were so old that I couldn't read what was written on them. It should have felt creepy, walking around a graveyard on my own, but it didn't. In a funny way, it felt kind of peaceful.

I wandered among the graves, not knowing where

to look. Then I stopped suddenly. There was a small stone cross, mostly covered with moss. At one edge, though, the moss was peeling off and I could read the beginning of a word – *Spi–*

I bent down and pulled away more of the moss. After a minute, the full inscription was revealed:

Bridget Spillane
March 1837–June 1912

I put my hands over my face.

Granny Bridget.

I thought of the gentle old lady who had been so kind to me, even though she had no idea who I was, or how I had suddenly appeared in her life.

I checked the date again. Granny Bridget had died just a few short months after I had been there.

Had Mikey made it safely back home? Did he stand on this very spot crying for his granny?

And whatever had happened to Mikey after his granny was gone? Did his father come back or was he left alone to care for himself?

Maybe none of this mattered now, so many years later, but still, I had to know.

I walked a bit further, half afraid to read the inscriptions on the headstones, but more afraid not to.

Then, in a shady corner, I found the stone I had been looking for.

Mikey Spillane
January 1901–May 2003

I breathed a huge long sigh of relief. He *had* made it back home safely.

My friend Mikey. It was weird to think that when I was a little girl, he was an ancient old man. Did he remember me? Did he ever think about the day we spent together in April 1912? And even though he lived such a long life, he never got to use the information I had given him about Spain winning the 2010 World Cup Final.

I leaned closer and noticed that there was more writing on the headstone, almost obscured by a thick layer of black stuff. I knelt down and set to work. I broke most of my fingernails as I scraped away the worst of the dirt. Then I took a tissue from my pocket and scrubbed until the tissue was shredded in my hand.

Then I stood back and read the inscription in full –

Mikey Spillane
January 1901–May 2003
Much loved and missed by his 6 sons, 4 daughters,
29 grandchildren and 17 great-grandchildren.

I could feel a slow smile spreading across my face.

So what if Mikey never got to make his fortune on the World Cup in 2010? He got to fill his house with children – the thing he wanted most of all in the world.

I wondered if Mikey told his grandchildren about his brief adventure on the *Titanic*. I wondered if he told them about me and if they checked up and discovered that no girl called Lauren had been on board the *Titanic*. Did they dismiss him as a crazy rambling old man – the way I had dismissed Betsy?

I picked a handful of daisies from the path and
laid them on the grave.

'So it all turned out well in the end, Mikey,' I said.
'I'm very glad for you.'

I checked to see that no one was around and I
patted his headstone with my hand. 'Goodbye,
Mikey,' I said, and then I turned to leave.

As I walked out of the graveyard, I saw a sign on
the railing.

DON'T FORGET TO CHECK OUT OUR EXHIBITION
IN THE CHURCH PORCH —
PHOTOGRAPHS FROM A FORGOTTEN AGE.

I walked quickly to the porch of the church. It
was a tiny space, but every inch of the walls had
been covered with faded old photographs. I scanned
them eagerly, but even though I searched every face,
there was no sign of Mikey or Granny Bridget.

I was just leaving, with a sick feeling of
disappointment, when something made me turn
back and look at one particular photograph. It was

212

a group of eight boys and girls and bore the caption
– BALLYBOHER NATIONAL SCHOOL, CONFIRMATION
DAY 1937.

All the children were smiling happily, but something about one girl seemed to be drawing me in.

I took a step closer.

It wasn't her blonde pigtails that caught my eye, or her laughing eyes. It wasn't her clumpy boots or her shapeless skirt. It was the neatly zipped fleece, with the logo I would know anywhere.

It had to be Mikey's daughter, wearing the first zipped fleece that had ever shown up in Ballyboher – the fleece that had travelled back in time and had even spent a few minutes on board the *Titanic*.

I was still laughing loudly as I walked back to the car. Mum wound down the window as I approached. Then she and Tilly exchanged looks again. They were *Oh-dear-now-she's-finally-gone-and-lost-it-completely* looks.

Tilly made a face at me. 'I take it you found that Bolivian revolution guy?'

213

I thought for a minute. I was getting tired of telling lies.

'Let's just say that I found exactly what I was looking for.'

'So can we go on to Cobh now?' said Mum.

'Yes, please,' I said as I opened the car door and threw myself into the front seat. 'Cobh sounds great.'

 **26**

'You know Susan thinks it's very odd that we didn't call on her first,' said Mum as the three of us climbed out of the car. 'She can't understand why we're spending the day in Cobh.'

'You can blame me,' I said. 'The family weirdo.'

Mum gave me a funny look.

Maybe I shouldn't have joked about it – maybe I really was turning into the freak of the family.

'I'm still starving,' said Tilly, tactfully changing the subject. 'Can we go for lunch?'

'Great idea,' agreed Mum, a bit too enthusiastically. 'Let's go this way.'

After a while she said, 'This is the harbour.'

But how could this be the harbour? Where were

the scurrying crowds? Where were the people
pushing and shoving? Why was everything so clean
and calm and quiet?

'But everything has changed,' I said, without
thinking.

Mum put her arm round me. 'Of course it's
changed,' she said. 'Everything changes with time.
But I don't know how you could know – you've
never been to Cobh before.'

I didn't answer. I could hardly say that Saturn
and I had been there a few days, or a few decades
before, depending on which way you chose to look
at it.

We found an Italian restaurant and I pretended
that I cared about any of the food on the menu.
When my giant pizza arrived, I said 'wow', as
convincingly as I could manage. During the meal,
Mum and Tilly did most of the talking and I
pretended to listen, like I was interested in a single
word they had to say.

After lunch the three of us stood outside the
restaurant.

'Well, girls,' said Mum. 'We have a few hours before Susan is expecting us. What do you want to do?'

'Go shopping and then go to the beach,' said Tilly.

'Go to the *Titanic* exhibition,' I said at the same time.

Mum and Tilly exchanged looks.

I'm not an expert on meaningful looks, but I was fairly sure it was a *Let's-pretend-not-to-notice-when-Lauren-does-something-strange* look.

I was wondering how I was going to explain my sudden interest in history, when Mum rescued me.

'How about we go to the *Titanic* exhibition and then to the beach?' she said, and no one could argue with that perfectly reasonable suggestion.

Mum and Tilly found the *Titanic* exhibition very interesting – for about five minutes.

'This place is OK,' said Tilly. 'But it's not half as good as the movie. This is basically just a lot of pictures of an old ship that sank.'

'But think about all the poor people who died,'

I said. 'Think of all the lives that were ruined. They were all real people with hopes and dreams – just like us.'

'Yeah, but that's ancient history,' said Tilly. 'Why should we care?'

'It's . . .' I started to say, but then I stopped. How could I even begin to explain the truth?

The sun was streaming through the windows. We were supposed to be on holiday and I knew I was being unfair.

'I know you've both seen enough of this place,' I said.

'How did you guess?' asked Tilly, yawning theatrically.

'Call it intuition,' I replied. 'Anyway, I'd love another bit of time here. Why don't you two go ahead and find a nice ice-cream shop and I'll catch up with you in a few minutes?'

'Are you sure?' said Mum uncertainly.

I nodded. 'Sure I'm sure.' I patted my jeans pocket. 'I've got my phone and I'll call you if I need you.'

So they went off and at last I was free to explore my strange, mixed-up past.

The room was small, but there were heaps of photographs of the *Titanic*. I examined each one like it might contain the secrets of the universe.

It was totally weird, looking at the faded black-and-white photos of what I had seen in such vivid colour only a few days before. The clothes of the women in First Class, which had been every shade from blue to orange to green, were now all turned to varying shades of black and white and grey.

There were lots of pictures of people in groups, but none of them included Mary or her mother or her cute little brother.

None of them included me.

I gasped as I came to the picture of the ship's captain. There he stood, all proud in his uniform. He looked cross and stern, but I remembered how he had been kind to me. He hadn't listened, but he had been nice in a funny, gruff way. I wondered if he remembered me when the ship began to go down?

Besides the photographs, there wasn't a whole lot to look at. There were a few letters, and five or six yellowing newspaper articles, and a single dinner menu saying RMS TITANIC in fading gold letters.

Why hadn't I filled my pockets with stuff, that last night on board the ship? I could have kept all kinds of interesting things that would have livened up this museum. But it's funny how you don't think of things like that when you are trying to save your life.

I wandered around for ages. I'm not sure what I was looking for, but I was sure I hadn't found it. I had the guilty thought that I was wrecking Mum and Tilly's afternoon for nothing.

It was time for me to give up on my strange yearning for the past and get back to the real world.

27

As I headed for the exit I noticed a rocking chair, with a model of an ancient old woman sitting in it.

Was she supposed to represent one of the *Titanic* passengers? If so, her clothes didn't look right. Maybe I should tell the museum people that no one on the *Titanic* had dressed like that.

I walked up to take a closer look at the model, and jumped when it moved.

'OMIGOD,' I shrieked. 'You're alive!'

'Well, I certainly hope so,' she said.

My heart was beating so fast I had to sit down before I fell down. Luckily there was a bench right next to us. As I recovered myself, I noticed that the woman was wearing an official-looking badge saying – *TITANIC* EXHIBITION.

She smiled. 'I've been watching you,' she said. 'We don't often get visitors who are as interested as you are. It's nice to see someone who looks as if she cares.'

'The *Titanic* is kind of like my specialist subject,' I said.

The woman looked impressed. 'And have you had that special interest in the *Titanic* for a long time?'

Well, ever since I found myself on it, actually.

She seemed to be waiting for a real answer. 'Well . . . since forever, really,' I said.

'That's nice,' she said. 'What's your name?'

'Lauren.'

'Well, well, what a funny coincidence. My name is Lauren too.'

'But . . .' I didn't know how to go on without sounding rude.

'I know. It's not an old woman's name. My mother loved it, though. She called me after a girl she knew long before I was born. She always used to say, "Lauren, I've given you the name of the girl who saved my life".'

I noticed that my breathing was speeding up. I felt slightly dizzy.

'What was your mother's name?' I asked faintly.

She laughed. 'My mother had the most popular name for girls at the time. Maybe that's why she gave me an unusual name. Being called Lauren was a bit inconvenient at times, I can tell you. No one ever knew how to spell it. Things are different now, since the name has become so popular, but back then –'

'And your mother's name was . . .?' I interrupted.

'Oh,' she said, looking embarrassed. 'I was rambling on a bit there – sorry. My mother's name was Mary.'

I was aware of my heart thumping in my chest. Was this a wild coincidence or was my imagination running ahead of me in huge leaps and bounds?

'Er . . . was your mother . . . was she . . . I mean . . . did she . . .?'

Lauren was waiting patiently for me to finish my sentence, but I couldn't do it. The words were just too hard.

She gave up waiting – time is probably precious when you get to her age. 'My mother was on the *Titanic*, you know,' she said. 'That's why I'm so interested in the whole subject. That's why I came to live in Ireland as soon as I retired.'

I put my hand on the edge of the seat to steady myself. 'And your mother . . . was she on her own on the *Titanic*?'

'Oh no. She was much too young to travel on her own. She was only a girl at the time.'

I'm only a girl and I was on the Titanic on my own.

Lauren continued. 'She was with her mother and her baby brother.'

'Baba.'

Now Lauren gave me a very strange look. 'He was christened Kevin, but the family always called him Baba, but I don't know how you could possibly know that.'

'Lucky guess,' I said weakly.

I thought of Baba's gummy smile and his gurgly laugh.

'And did they all . . .?'

Lauren smiled. 'Oh, they all survived. They were very lucky.'

'And did your mother ever tell you *how* they survived?'

Lauren shook her head slowly. 'My mother never would talk about it. I think a lot of the *Titanic* survivors were like that. It was a horrific experience and they just wanted to forget.'

'So you've no idea how . . .?'

'How they managed to get off the boat, when so many of the other passengers died?'

I nodded.

'I've always thought that it must be something to do with that girl Lauren. It makes sense, after all, since my mother said that Lauren saved her life. But no matter how often I asked her, she'd just smile and say, "It's all in the past. I'm glad I got a second chance at life".'

She gave a big sigh. 'When I was a little girl, I

225

used to wish that I could meet that first Lauren. I had this crazy dream that one day I could travel back in time, so I could talk to her for a few minutes.'

'Be careful what you wish for,' I muttered.

She didn't hear me.

'I'm never going to meet her now,' she continued. 'She must have died years ago.'

Well, actually, no. I'm alive and well and standing in front of you.

But how could I say that? *How weird would that be?*

And speaking of weird, how come Mary was still a young girl, in my mind, while her daughter was already an old lady?

Then I remembered something else. 'When your mother grew up – did she get to design hats?'

Now Lauren looked even closer at me.

'What funny questions you ask,' she said. 'You're a strange little girl. Has anyone ever told you that before?'

I shook my head. No one ever told me that before, because, until recently I was a very ordinary girl, not some weirdo who goes around asking questions about stuff that happened a few life-times ago.

'But what about the hats?' I prompted her.

Lauren smiled. 'My mother told me once that her childhood dream was to become a hat designer.'

'And?'

'Well, sometimes childhood dreams are just that – dreams. My mother married young and then stayed at home with us kids – there were five of us. Then, when we were all grown up, she went back to school and trained as a doctor. When my father died, she went to Africa and worked in a hospital that helped children who were in danger of going blind. She saved hundreds of children from a life of complete darkness. The government gave her a big reward in recognition of what she had done.'

'You must have been very proud of her,' I said.

Lauren smiled again. 'I was. My mother loved helping people. She did a lot of good in her life.'

'And is she . . .?' I couldn't finish the question, but Lauren was getting good at understanding my half-questions.

'My mother had a long life,' she said. 'She died when she was eighty-five.'

I did a quick sum in my head. That would have been before I was even born.

'And was she happy?'

Lauren didn't hesitate. 'Yes. She was the happiest woman I ever knew. And know what?'

'What?'

'She always wore the prettiest hats. She trimmed all of her hats with lace and feathers and pearls. "A lady is never fully dressed without a hat," she used to say.'

I knew from the Internet that most of the Third-Class passengers on the *Titanic* died, but Mary and her family had survived. And maybe, just maybe, it was all because of me.

It was time for me to go. I stood up and put out my hand, ready to shake Lauren's, just as I had done with her mother, days or decades ago.

Lauren leaned forward to take my hand and for the first time I could see the silver charm that was dangling from a chain round her neck.

'What's that round your neck?'

Lauren beamed. 'It's pretty, isn't it? It was my mother's.'

I know that already – I'm the one who gave it to her.

Lauren twisted the charm thoughtfully.

'It says –'

'Friends Forever.' I finished the sentence for her and she gave me yet another strange look.

'When I was growing up, this was most unusual,' she said. 'Everyone used to comment on it. But now, all of a sudden, this kind of thing is the height of fashion. Funny, isn't it? Maybe some jewellery designer noticed me wearing this sometime and copied it.'

'Maybe,' I said with a vague smile.

I shook Lauren's old hand in mine and then I turned and headed for the door.

'Wait.'

I turned to see her hurrying towards me. She was holding something small in her hand. 'I see you collect charms,' she said.

'I do, but . . .'

She put the small metal object into my hand and I saw that it was a tiny ship.

'The *Titanic*,' she said. 'It's a perfect replica. It's the only one left over from a promotion we were doing last week, and I'd like you to have it.'

'But why –'

'Because if I don't give it to you, it will probably end up being given to the very spoiled child of the museum manager. And . . .'

She hesitated and I watched as a dreamy look came over her face.

'And?' I prompted.

'Because giving it to you feels right in a way that I can't, for the life of me, understand.'

There were a lot of things I didn't understand, either.

I looked at the tiny ship in my hand.

'It will look nice on your charm bracelet,' said Lauren.

'It will look perfect!' I said.

And we both smiled.

*

There was a low wall outside the museum and I sat there for a minute, enjoying the sunshine and trying to gather my thoughts.

Pictures of Mary and Mikey raced through my head. Mikey got the big family he had dreamed of, and Mary got all she wished for in America.

Then a very strange thought struck me.

What if Betsy hadn't given me her cat?

What if Mikey had insisted on doing his jobs, and hadn't brought me to Queenstown that afternoon?

What if Ernestine hadn't put Saturn into her basket?

I would never have been on the *Titanic*. So what would have happened to Mary? What would have happened to all the little children whose sight she saved? How could those small acts have changed so many lives?

I wasn't sure I fully understood what had happened to me, but all of a sudden I felt happier than I had in a long time. It was as if the dark cloud that had been following me around for days had floated far away. A warm, happy feeling washed over me and I started to laugh.

I found Mum and Tilly sitting outside a small cafe.

'Everything OK?' asked Mum as I approached.

I gave her a big grin.

'Everything's perfect,' I said, feeling very guilty at how happy those words seemed to make her.

I raised my arm to show her my bracelet.

'Look,' I said. 'There was a really nice woman in there and she gave me a present of a *Titanic* charm.'

Mum shook her head. 'You and your charms,' she said. 'Soon that bracelet will be too heavy for you to wear.'

Something in her eyes made me feel sad. I knew she was glad to be teasing me about jewellery instead of listening to me fretting about museums and falling-down houses and dreams that couldn't possibly be true.

Tilly was just finishing an ice cream. 'Sorry, Lauren,' she said. 'This was meant for you – but it was melting.'

I watched as Tilly delicately licked the last traces of ice cream from the spoon and I suddenly remembered the day, weeks earlier, when she and I had been eating ice creams in my back garden. The day I had dreamed of making a difference to the world.

And in a very roundabout way, my dream had come true.

Tilly looked up and noticed me watching her.

'What?' she asked.

I hesitated. I wasn't ready to tell her the whole story just yet.

'What?' she asked again.

'Oh, nothing,' I said. 'Nothing at all.'

'So we can go to the beach now?' asked Tilly, jumping up from her seat.

I nodded. 'Bring it on.'

It all started with a Scarecrow.

Puffin is seventy years old.
Sounds ancient, doesn't it? But Puffin has never been
so lively. We're always on the lookout for the next big
idea, which is how it began all those years ago.

Penguin Books was a big idea from the mind of
a man called Allen Lane, who in 1935 invented
the quality paperback and changed the world.
**And from great Penguins, great Puffins grew,
changing the face of children's books forever.**

The first four Puffin Picture Books were hatched in 1940 and the
first Puffin story book featured a man with broomstick arms called
Worzel Gummidge. In 1967 Kaye Webb, Puffin Editor, started the
Puffin Club, promising to **'make children into readers'**.
She kept that promise and over 200,000 children became
devoted Puffineers through their quarterly instalments of
Puffin Post, which is now back for a new generation.

Many years from now, we hope you'll look back and
remember Puffin with a smile. **No matter what your age
or what you're into, there's a Puffin for everyone.**
The possibilities are endless, but one thing is for sure:
whether it's a picture book or a paperback, a sticker book
or a hardback, **if it's got that little Puffin
on it – it's bound to be good.**